/ / JAN 2003

Class No. 5

Acc No. C/62073

Author: SCOTT, M.

Loc. / / SEP 1996

1. **This book may be kept three weeks.
   It is to be returned on / before the last date
   stamped below.**
2. **A fine of 20p will be charged for every week
   or part of week a book is overdue.**

VAMPYRE

Vampyre

Michael Scott

POOLBEG

Published in 1995
by Poolbeg Press Ltd
123 Baldoyle Industrial Estate
Dublin 13, Ireland

Reprinted December 1995

© Michael Scott 1995

The moral right of the authors has been asserted.

A catalogue record for this book is available from the British Library.

ISBN 1 85371 545 X

Cover illustration by Peter Haigh
Cover design by Poolbeg Group Services Ltd
Set by Poolbeg Group Services Ltd in Times
Printed by The Guernsey Press Ltd,
Vale, Guernsey, Channel Islands.

A note on the author

Michael Scott is an internationally renowned writer. He has written over forty books. *Vampyre* is his first novel for Poolbeg.

For Karen

who bears no resemblance to anyone in this book

and

for Nicole

PROLOGUE

The creature was still alive when we put it in the ground. I chose six men, all veteran warriors without families, to bury the foul creature, for I knew it would be a dangerous and possibly deadly undertaking. We took the thing out of its cell at noon, when its powers were weakest, but even then we handled it warily, knowing its small size and feminine appearance belied a supernatural strength.

Its screams were terrifying, the very sound another of the creature's weapons, the noise rising higher than human hearing, until the ears and nostrils of the warriors streamed blood and their faces were drawn with pain. Four struggled to hold the beast, one on each arm and leg, while the remaining two fought to manoeuvre the wriggling creature into the stone casket.

Once, twice, the thing almost escaped, lashing out with a foot to send one of the men crashing to the ground with shattered ribs, twisting its head to snap at the hand of another, razor sharp teeth almost tearing off two fingers. Finally, when it looked as if the creature might prevail, Father Patrick dashed forward and doused the thing with blessed oil and holy water. Ghastly pale flesh hissed and bubbled where the sacred liquids touched it, and the beast began twisting and spasming. I ran forward, wrapped my metal-gloved hands in the creature's hair and held its head steady while he applied more oil and water. As it writhed in agony and beat at the smouldering spots on its body touched by the blessed oil, we threw the squirming creature into the coffin.

The priest rained holy water on to the creature while we manoeuvred the lid into place. Four men, heavy in leather and metal armour, sat on the lid to hold it down while the blacksmith affixed chains and rivets. But even with that weight atop the heavy stone lid the beast still managed to shift it and I clearly saw its yellow eyes glaring at me through the tiny opening. With a tremendous effort we settled the lid back in place. The blacksmith then filled the seam where the coffin lid joined the body of the casket with molten lead, and Father Patrick inscribed the names of the Archangels into the hardening metal. We then lowered the coffin deep into the ground. Rather than filling the pit with earth, we brought rocks from the nearby quarry and tossed these into the opening. More lead was poured over the rocks and mortar, such as masons use to hold stones together, was poured over that.

Then, and only then, when the beast was encased in solid stone and buried deep beneath the earth, did I breathe easily.

The devil-beast was condemned to an eternity of imprisonment. It would not escape in my lifetime or in my children's lifetime. Perhaps in some distant age, when mankind has advanced in knowledge and learning, it will know how to deal with the creature the Irish call the *Bobhan Sith*.

CHAPTER ONE

He still missed her.

Robert Carroll pulled the left brake lever, worn brake blocks squeaking off the metal wheel rim, and then hopped off the bike while it was still moving.

She had been dead a year and he still missed her.

He'd been surprised by his own reaction. Aunt Maggie was old, and old people died, so he should not have been so surprised. But she had been such a part of his childhood and youth. When his mother had spent six months in hospital following the car accident, it had been Aunt Maggie who had taken care of him; when his father had spent a year working in England, it had been Aunt Maggie whom he had gone to live with.

But then, as so often happens in families, Aunt Maggie had simply drifted away and out of the family circle. Robert wasn't sure exactly why or how it had happened. She had gone from practically living in the house, to calling twice a week, and then it was once a week, or twice a month, until finally it was once a year, and by that time she was almost a stranger. In the last five years, he doubted if he'd seen her five times, and they had barely spoken, stiff, stilted conversations between a teenager and a woman in her eighties. He had grown up and she had grown old, and they had simply grown apart.

And yet when he had discovered that she was ill in hospital, he'd felt as if someone had just kicked him in the pit of the stomach, and suddenly there were tears in his eyes and acid in his throat. He felt guilty. He'd visited her only once, and the sight of the old, withered woman in the bed – surely this couldn't be his aunt? – had upset him badly. And when he'd learned of her death two days after his visit, the depth of his pain had shocked and surprised him.

Robert had read the lesson in church, a piece from the *Book of Ecclesiastes*, "There is a season for all things." From the very first words, he had been racing to see if he would be able to finish before he broke down. He'd managed it – barely.

Now he had come to visit her.

Hefting the heavy mountain bike up on to his shoulder, he climbed over the stile into the field.

Aunt Maggie had been buried in Baldungan Cemetery in Loughshinny where she'd lived all her life. The tiny graveyard was attached to the remains of a tumbled thirteenth century church and castle, which was accessible across a field sown with potatoes. The church and graveyard were surrounded by a low wall and there was

4

only a scattering of new headstones in the graveyard, most were old and a few were ancient. The castle was now nothing more than a tower, still in remarkably good repair, standing at one end of a shell of the equally ancient church. The roof of the church was gone and a portion of one wall was missing, but the thickness of the walls testified to the strength of the fortifications. As he walked across the hard-packed strip of bare earth that cut through the green field, Robert wondered whom it had been built to protect.

Lifting his bike across the metal gates, he climbed over into the churchyard. Usually he would walk through the church, step out through the hole in the wall into the graveyard. But the church floor was covered with pebbles and dragging the bike through would cause a terrible racket. He was reluctant to disturb the morning's stillness. Leaving the bike propped up against the wall, he strolled slowly around the perimeter wall, hands dug deep into the pockets of his faded, cut-off jeans. He shivered as he passed beneath the shadow of the tower; it was still early enough to be chill out of the sunlight, but the day promised to be a scorcher. He stopped as he came around the side of the church, and stared out across the sloping fields towards the distant sea where Lambay Island was clearly visible in the distance.

When he could put it off no longer, he turned to look at Aunt Maggie's grave. It had only been three days, but already the fresh flowers had withered in the brilliant

August sunshine, and the piled earth was dried and cracked. Kneeling on the grassy margin, he started to gather up the flowers in their plastic and paper wrappers. They came with the little tag cards similar to those put on gifts. He didn't know any of the people; they were like those people who had come up to his parents in church or at the graveyard and shook hands with them. He was sure his mother or father would not remember any of them. But they all knew his aunt.

The Family of . . .

Betty, Jimmy and . . .

From everyone in . . .

Robert pulled the tags off the dead flowers and placed them under a stone to prevent them from blowing away. Gathering up the flowers and paper in his arms, he carried them to the metal bin and dumped them inside. Returning to the graveside, he knelt down and began sorting through the cards, reading aloud the names. Who were these people, and why had they sent flowers? Did they send them because they thought they should, or had they sent them because they genuinely missed the old woman?

He hadn't sent flowers . . . and yet he missed her.

And he couldn't explain why.

Maybe it was because she was the first member of his family, someone he knew, who had died. He was sixteen – seventeen shortly – and although he had attended funerals in school, or those his parents had dragged him along to, it had never been anyone he knew. But Aunt Maggie was . . . family.

Robert stood up, shuffling the cards in his hands and looking at the piled earth. Maybe it was the sudden realisation that one day he would be looking down at the grave of his own mother or father; the awareness that one day he too would die. He smiled nervously, thin lips twisting. He'd read somewhere that the first true sign of adulthood was understanding that you were not going to live forever.

"I'll come back tomorrow," he said softly as he turned away.

He was pushing the cards in the pocket of his jeans when one tumbled away, spinning to the ground, disappearing into a tuft of grass. Sighing, he bent to pick it up, searching through the grass. The sudden sting felt cold, then hot pain flooded along the palm of his hand.

Robert swore and yanked his hand back. A triangular sliver of glass protruded from the centre of his palm, which was now gushing blood. Blinking away tears of pain, he gingerly caught the glass between forefinger and thumb of his left hand and eased it out of his flesh. His hand was throbbing in agony. The glass had cut him from just below the middle finger to the soft pad at the base of his thumb. Holding his hand down, he pressed hard on the skin with his left hand, urging it to bleed more, ensuring that it would wash out any infection – Aunt Maggie had taught him that. Bright red blood dripped from his fingers and splashed on to the grass, curling off the broken glass of the ornamental plastic flowers that lay half hidden in the grass. Pulling a grubby paper hankie from his pocket, he wrapped it around the gash, and turned away. He was wondering how he was going to lift the heavy mountain bike over the low wall with only one hand.

CHAPTER TWO

B*lood.*
Warm and red, it seeped through the crusted earth, running along the sun-baked cracks, finding its way through tiny crevices.

Blood.

Rich and dark, the tiny rivulet of blood sank deeper into the ancient soil. It soaked through dried mud, coated pebbles, oozed past slates and shells, until it finally touched the edge of a massive stone that was too regular to be natural. The blood, now thinned by its journey, crept along the edge of the stone, then sank through the tiny crevices . . . and dripped.

On to flesh.

Old flesh, ancient flesh, encasing a skull.

The last droplet of the boy's blood nestled almost delicately against a sunken cheek.

Until the pointed tongue flickered out.

And drank, lapping it up.

CHAPTER THREE

"I think it needs a stitch." Joyce Carroll turned the cold tap on full, allowing the icy water to blast on to Robert's torn hand.

"Aw, don't say that, Mum."

"Maybe even a tetanus shot," she added with a comforting smile.

Robert attempted to jerk his hand away, but his mother had it caught in a vice-like grip. He had gashed his leg last summer on a piece of barbed wire and had to have it stitched and have a tetanus jab. He hadn't been able to sit down for a week.

"What did you cut it on?" she demanded.

"Grass," he said through clenched teeth. "I think," he added. He wouldn't need a tetanus if he'd cut himself on grass.

"You think," Joyce said slowly, patting at the torn skin with a pad of kitchen paper. "It looks too deep for a grass cut."

"Might have been glass," he admitted. "Maybe there was a broken bottle or something in the long grass."

"Glass." She poured disinfectant on to the cut and he

hissed in pain, rising up on to his toes. "Are you sure there wasn't any metal around?"

"I don't think so."

"Are you even sure it was glass?" she continued to question him.

"Well, it certainly looked like glass when I pulled it out of my skin," he snapped, then immediately realised his mistake.

"I thought you said it was grass!"

"It was glass," he admitted.

"Then I certainly think you should have a tetanus."

Robert protested, "But it was glass, not metal."

Frowning in concentration, Joyce pressed a gauze pad to the cut and taped up the edges. The centre of the cloth swiftly turned pink. "How long ago did this happen?"

Robert lifted his left arm . . . and discovered, with a sinking feeling in the pit of his stomach, that his watch was missing. "About . . . half an hour ago," he said, hastily dropping his arm before she noticed too.

The watch had been a Christmas present from his parents; one hundred and twenty pounds worth of hi-tech digital wizardry, it could tell the time in twenty-one countries, was waterproof, dustproof, solar powered, accurate to a thousandth of a second. The case of the watch was silver, but he'd replaced the silvery strap with a leather one; the metal strap kept nicking and pulling the short hairs on his wrist. The leather strap must have broken and fallen off his wrist in the graveyard.

"Your father will be back in a couple of minutes," his mother continued. "If it hasn't stopped bleeding by then, I'll have him take you into Casualty and let them have a look at it. Now, go upstairs and lie down until he gets back."

"But it's only a cut . . ."

"Any deeper and it would have come out the other side of your hand. When I was a girl . . ."

Robert groaned silently. His mother had a load of stories about people she had grown up with; most of them seemed either to have injured themselves horrifically through their own carelessness or had all the diseases known to man. He had long ago come to the conclusion that all his mother's friends were really unlucky. "This isn't the girl who lost her finger because she stuck a pin in it?"

"No, that was Mary Whelan," his mother said immediately, unaware that Robert was trying to be sarcastic. "But she had a friend, Maureen Moore, and she got lockjaw from sitting on a rusty nail."

Not quite sure of the connection between sitting on a nail and getting lockjaw – and he wasn't entirely sure what lockjaw was – he decided not to pursue the matter further. "I think I'll go and lie down," he said, leaving the kitchen and closing the door behind him. He clumped heavily down the hall and stamped up the stairs, making sure to put his full weight on all the stairs which creaked. When he reached the landing he stopped, however, and leaned over the banisters to listen. He could hear his mother moving about in the kitchen below and then the back door opened, hinges protesting loudly. After that there was silence.

He slipped into his parents' bedroom and crossed to the window which looked down into the orchard below.

Most of the trees were in fruit and the smell of apples rose through the open window, the scent rich and strong, one of those odours that immediately made him think of Aunt Maggie. Peering through the canopy of leaves, he saw his mother setting up the deckchair in the shade of one of the older trees. He turned his head to look at the clock on the bedside locker.

Three-fifteen.

His mother had said that his father would be back in a couple of minutes, but Robert knew he had gone into Dublin less than an hour ago. It was at least a forty minute drive to the city, another forty minutes returning, and even if he only spent twenty minutes in the city, that still meant he would be gone for at least another forty minutes. Plenty of time to return to the ruined church and look for his watch.

CHAPTER FOUR

He noticed the movement as he pushed the bike across the field: a flash of red against the grey stone, brilliant by comparison with the parched fields beyond. It had been an unusually dry summer.

Robert slowed and stopped, unwilling to disturb anyone in the graveyard, knowing how he would feel in similar circumstances. Should he make a noise, let them know he was coming, or perhaps just slip away . . . ?

Another flicker of red resembled a crimson scarf whipping in the wind . . . but there was no wind.

Curious now, he left his bike on the path, and approached the castle slowly, sneakers making no sound on the baked earth, grey eyes squinting against the glare of the early afternoon sun. When he reached the low wall surrounding the graveyard he stopped, head tilted to one side, listening. But the air was still and silent. Maybe he'd been imagining it . . .

On the opposite side of the ruined chapel, stones rattled.

And then he heard, thin and high on the summer air, the sound of a young woman sobbing.

Robert felt tears start to his own eyes; he had never

heard so much pain in a voice before. Trotting through the gate, he followed the path around by the wall to the left.

Later, all he could remember were impressions of colours: a young woman's white face, startlingly pale, eyes bright and green, lips red, brilliant red hair. . .

And then the girl was up and running, darting among the tumbled gravestones and racing around to the other side of the ruined castle. Instinctively Robert followed her, but by the time he reached the opposite side of the graveyard she had vanished. Robert climbed on to the wall, shading his eyes with his hands, turning to look across the fields, but there was no sign of the girl. Nor was there any shelter nearby where she might be hiding. Surely it hadn't taken him that long to run around the chapel . . .

Shaking his head, he returned to the spot where he'd seen the young woman. Alongside the piled earth that marked his aunt's new grave, the earth was sunken and scattered in the shape of a shallow pit. In the dry, dusty earth, the imprint of her hand stood out clearly. Robert crouched and spread his own hand alongside the imprint in the earth. The girl's hand was smaller, but the fingers were longer. He was still looking at it when the edges of the impression crumbled away, taking the imprint of her hand, and all trace of the girl, with it.

What was she doing here? Who was she? When he'd first come upon her, it had looked – for a brief moment – as if she had been digging. He smiled, shaking his head; maybe his mother was right, maybe he had an overactive imagination. Kneeling alongside the grave, he carefully parted the long grass, looking for his lost watch.

Silver glinted in the shadows.

Relieved, Robert shoved his hand into the thick of the grass, taking care not to slice open his hand on the razor-sharp blades. He was expecting to feel the smooth metal or glass of his watch; instead his questing fingers touched what felt like moulded plastic. One of those horrible plastic flowers, he thought, hooking it out.

It was a comb. About six inches long, a semi-circle, without a handle, as broad as his palm. The nine tines, thick where they were set into the body of the comb, narrowed to razor points. The body of the comb had been elaborately etched with curling, swirling symbols: tiny bird, animal and human faces. Although it looked as if it had been made from yellowed plastic, Robert instinctively knew that this was older, much older. He tapped the comb against the palm of his hand; it felt cool, like bone. Tilting the comb to the sunlight, he brought it close to his face, squinting to look closely at the material. The yellow-white surface was pitted with thousands of tiny holes, some of which were clogged with hard-packed earth. It *was* bone. A bone comb. He was wondering who it belonged to when he noticed the single red hair caught between two of the teeth. Untangling the hair, he laid it across the palm of his hand and looked at it. In the afternoon sunlight, it burned like a thread of blood.

CHAPTER FIVE

Karen O'Sullivan shook her head, pushing strands of ash blond hair off her high forehead. "I know no one who fits that description," she said decisively.

"Think again," Robert urged her. "She'd be about your age – fifteen or so – though sometimes when I think about her again, I get the impression that she was older, much older, early twenties perhaps."

Karen punched him quickly on the arm. "Hey, I'm not sure I like the idea of you thinking about other girls." She stepped closer to Robert and steered him up the beach, away from the incoming tide. She didn't want to get her new Nike sneakers wet; salt water would stain them permanently.

"I can't help thinking about her," said Robert. His voice was very serious. "You didn't hear her cry. It was so . . . sad."

Karen hooked her arm through Robert's. Although she was slightly younger than he, she was much taller, which occasionally embarrassed her. She was the tallest girl in her class, the tallest in her year, and she still hadn't stopped growing. She reckoned she'd top six feet before her sixteenth birthday. Over the years she had developed several tricks for dealing with her height; she tended to wear flat shoes, or keep her head and shoulders hunched, or, like now, walk on the lower slope of the beach. It wasn't so bad going out with Robert, but when she'd been going with Tommy Doolan, who had been a lot shorter, the others in the class had nicknamed them Little and Large.

"Was she pretty, that girl you saw?" she asked suddenly.

Robert thought for a moment before replying. He had caught only a glimpse of the girl. She was startling-looking, certainly, with that flaming red hair and pale complexion . . . but pretty? He wasn't sure. There had been something about her face, though, something he'd noticed and then forgotten as he tried to catch up with her. Perhaps her mouth had been too large, her eyes too small and set too close together?

"No, Karen," he said finally, "I don't think she could be called pretty. But you'd notice her if you saw her in the village."

"I know every girl of that age in Skerries, Loughshinny, Rush, Lusk and Balbriggan, and I assure you that no one fitting that description lives around here. There are any number of redheads of course, but none of them has lost any relatives recently." She took the comb from Robert's hands. "And I've never seen anything like this before, either. It looks really old . . ."

"Look at the design work," Robert said, tilting the comb to catch the last purple-red rays of the setting sun. It threw the etching into high relief, picking out the intricate details. "This must be ancient."

"Where do you think it came from?"

Robert shook his head. He'd asked himself that question a hundred times during the afternoon, and so far he'd failed to come up with any explanation.

"Maybe that red-haired girl dropped it?" Karen suggested.

"Maybe. But if you had something this old would you be carrying it around with you?"

"Could be it's not that old after all."

"It is, though," Robert said decisively. "I know it is."

"Well," replied Karen, looking away so he wouldn't see the smile on her face. "It's very easy to lose things."

Robert sighed. "I know. I know. Don't remind me. I haven't found my watch, and it's only a matter of time before my parents notice it's missing."

"What are you going to do?"

"It has to be in the graveyard. I'm going to get up early in the morning and go back to look for it."

"I'll meet you there, OK? What time?"

"Nine?"

"I'll see you then." Karen glanced at her own watch. "I'd better be heading back home."

"Here." Robert pressed the ancient comb into her hands. "You keep this."

The girl looked at it in surprise, uncertain whether to be pleased or not; she wasn't sure she wanted some tatty old comb Robert had picked up in a graveyard, of all places.

Catching her fingers in both his hands, he folded them around the comb. "It just might be really valuable," he told her. "If it is, I want you to have it." Then he ran one hand across his close-cropped hair and smiled ruefully. "I really don't have much use for a comb."

CHAPTER SIX

Karen O'Sullivan stood in front of the bedroom window and looked down towards the sea. Her parents had recently moved into a new bungalow built on a rise overlooking the beach and most of the town of Skerries. Karen hated the bungalow, which still stank of paint and new carpet and wet plaster, but she loved the view.

Her bedroom at the back of the house had two large windows, one facing north towards the town, the other looking down on to the beach. At night, with the town lit up and sparkling, it was magical. She could see the glittering lights of the amusement arcade at the far end of the seafront, and the ferris wheel outlined with coloured bulbs.

Usually, however, she preferred the view on to the beach. Tonight, with the moon high in the heavens, the sand was black, the sea shimmering like painted metal and the surf looking like silver mercury. The three islands, Colt, Patrick and Shenick, appeared like silhouette cut-outs against the horizon. She pushed open the window and breathed in the cool salt air.

It was so still, so silent.

Noise; that was what she really missed about her old house, she decided. They had lived in an estate on the edge of Skerries, in the middle of a block of semi-detached houses. She had been born in that house, grown up there, knew everyone and could recognise all the noises. At night, as she lay in bed, she could identify which doors were opening, whose car was turning into the estate, who was shovelling coal, she could even tell people by the sound of footsteps in the street outside. But here there was nothing except the vague hiss of the sea, like a great beast breathing, or the distant crying of gulls, sounding unpleasantly like children crying. Even the house was still. The old house creaked and groaned, stairs sighed when you stood on them, doors complained, the television aerial on the roof rattled in the slightest breeze, the water-tank in the attic gurgled softly like a cat purring. Here the walls were so thick and well-insulated that it was impossible to hear sounds from the other rooms. She had grown up listening to the music and voices on the television percolating up from below, the tinny hissing of the radio in her elder brother's room, the chirpy music from her younger sister's tape recorder. Often she claimed they drove her mad, but they had been comforting too, telling her that she wasn't alone, others were close by.

Now, when she stepped into her bedroom and closed the door, it was as if she had cut off the rest of the world.

She hated this place.

Sighing, Karen turned away from the window and sat down before her dressing table. She flicked on the table lamp, blinking hard as the sudden light hurt her eyes. When she could see again, she looked into the mirror and made a face, then leaned forward, tilting her head to the left to look at her cheek. Was that a spot?

Sighing, she sorted through the mess on the dressing table looking for cotton wool and cleansing milk. She knew she shouldn't have had that Mars bar, she told herself as she poured the white liquid on to the cotton wool and rubbed at her face, shocked when the cotton wool came away black. When she had finished cleaning her face, the wicker basket under the dressing table overflowed with cotton balls. Picking up her brush, she attempted to drag it through her blond hair. It caught and snagged, tugging at her hair with enough force to bring tears to her eyes. Frustrated, she flung the brush across the room. It bounced off her bed and thumped on to the floor. Her hair was a mess; it was too long and too fine to manage easily. She'd been thinking about having it chopped; maybe even getting a Number Two or Three, a bit like Robert's haircut. But she knew her parents would have a fit if she came home with a skinhead haircut. They would probably stop her from seeing Robert.

She lifted the comb he had given her. The teeth were long and fine, thick at the base, tapering to narrow points . . . it looked as if it had been made for long hair.

Carrying the comb over to the sink – all the bedrooms in the new bungalow had en-suite bathrooms – she twisted the hot water tap and filled the basin. She turned the comb over and over in her hands while debating whether to drop it into the water or not – would hot water harm it? Then, deciding that if it had lain in the ground for years there was probably very little that could harm it, Karen dropped the comb into the water. It floated for a few seconds, then sank in a stream of bubbles.

Using the expensive liquid soap that came in pump top bottles, she squirted some on to the comb, then worked it into the cracks with an old toothbrush.

Fifteen minutes later, having changed the filthy water three times, she was looking at a truly gorgeous object. Cleansed of its covering of mud and encrusted dirt, the comb was beautiful. The curling, swirling designs of tiny birds, abstract animal shapes and large-eyed human faces were clearer now, woven together into an intricate Celtic pattern that drew the eyes, making her follow the individual lines with open-mouthed admiration. How very beautiful it was! The half moon shape fit easily into the palm of her hand, and it seemed the most natural thing in the world to do to draw it through her hair.

The narrow teeth parted the tangled strands easily, separating them as her hair crackled with static electricity. When she lifted the comb away from her head, strands of blond hair rose, waving and shimmering, after it. Staring into the mirror, Karen pulled the comb through her hair in long even strokes, wondering how something this old could work so easily when the modern plastic combs made combing her hair such a nightmare. This comb had been made by primitive people . . . but they had known a lot more about hair than modern comb designers.

Tilting her face to the ceiling, allowing her hair to tumble down her back, she placed the comb at her temples and drew it downwards in long even strokes. Straightening up, she turned her face to one side, brushing the hair back . . .

. . . and saw another face in the mirror.

Her startled shriek turned to a cry of pain as the needle-sharp teeth of the comb bit into the soft flesh of her neck.

Karen spun around, heart thundering, holding the comb before her like a weapon, but the room was empty. She had been so certain she'd seen a face reflected in the mirror, but even now, a split second later, as she tried to recall what it looked like, she found that the details were fading. She thought the face had belonged to a girl . . . a red-haired girl.

She was just over-tired, she told herself sternly as she turned back to the mirror. Pulling down her collar, she examined her neck where the comb had bitten into her. There were four long scratches along the left side of her neck ending in two puncture marks. When she looked at the wounds again, she couldn't help wondering why they hadn't bled. Lifting the comb and holding it close to her face, she was surprised to discover that there was no blood on the tines.

CHAPTER SEVEN

The call of blood.

Powerful.

Demanding.

It heard the call of blood, the powerful pulse that was at the core of every living creature.

A call that had sustained it, nurtured it.

A call it had not heard in an age, and yet – today – it had heard the call twice. The first had awakened it, a tiny drop of liquid, a spark of fire illuminating the endless night of sleep. It had waited . . . waited for the call, knowing it would come.

Then it followed the red threads of the call back toward their source.

CHAPTER EIGHT

Robert was sitting on the low wall surrounding the graveyard when Karen came puffing up. The girl was red-faced, cheeks glowing, blond hair plastered close to her skull, her forehead gleaming with sweat, a soaking *Take That* tee-shirt stuck to her skin.

"You're out of condition," he grinned.

Karen nodded, unable to speak. Leaning her bike against the wall, she bent double with her hands on her knees and breathed in great gulps of the cool morning air. This morning, the cycle down from Skerries to Loughshinny – a trip she made two or three times a week without any ill-effects – had left her exhausted, her legs feeling like rubber, acid churning in her stomach, bile burning at the back of her throat. When she straightened up, Robert's smile faded and was replaced by a look of concern. "Are you OK?" Karen's face was pale, no colour in her cheeks, and there were dark semi-circles beneath her eyes.

"I think I'm coming down with something. Hay-fever, maybe."

"I didn't know you suffered from hay-fever."

"I don't usually."

"I hope it's not one of those summer colds; they can take forever to get rid of."

Karen nodded miserably. She had spent the night tossing and turning, alternating between feeling too hot, then shivering with a chill. Twice, she awoke from a deep sleep with remnants of nightmares flitting away as she opened her eyes. She couldn't remember anything about the dreams, except that they had been disturbing.

"You should not have come," Robert told her, sounding concerned.

"I'll be fine." She attempted a smile, which failed. "Come on, let's have a look for this watch of yours."

With a shrug, Robert hopped over the low wall. Normally Karen would have followed his route, but this morning she contented herself with pushing through the revolving gate. She joined the boy beside the ruined chapel, beneath the shadow of the tower.

She had always thought this a particularly cold spot, and in spite of the summery weather, today it felt almost icy. The morning air was tainted with the odour of slurry from the surrounding farms. In the distance, across the patchwork of fields dotted with houses, she could see Lambay Island wreathed in mist, and although the sky above her head was cloudless, a delicate eggshell blue, the distant city of Dublin was shrouded in grey cloud.

"Here," Robert said, drawing her attention. He was kneeling down, pointing to a patch of disturbed earth. "I think I dropped it here." With his uninjured hand, he carefully parted the long grass.

Karen knelt beside him, bare knees poking through her worn jeans. "I've brought some of my father's gardening tools. There're in the bag on my bike. Would you get them for me, please?"

While Robert went for the bag, Karen examined the ground, looking for any tell-tale glint of metal. This spot, in the shadow of the tower, was the oldest part of the cemetery. A few of the graves here went back two hundred years, and she'd read somewhere that there were even older headstones buried in the soft earth beneath them. She knew that the original church was supposed to have been built in the thirteenth century and used for centuries afterwards. It had stood abandoned and in ruins for at least the last two hundred years.

Robert reappeared and knelt beside her, opening the bag and lifting out a small fork and a spade. "I would never have thought of bringing these," he admitted.

Karen grinned as she took the fork from Robert's hand and plunged it into the earth. One of the reasons she liked Robert was because he was not afraid to admit that she was smarter than he was. So many of the boys that she'd gone out with liked to think that they were cleverer than she was, and never gave her credit for anything. With an effort, she turned over the top layer of earth. "You're sure this is where you lost the watch?"

"Well, if I was sure, it wouldn't be lost . . . would it? You can't lose something if you know where it is," he said reasonably.

Karen shook her head. It was too early in the morning for such complicated thinking. She dug up another spadeful of soil, surprised to find that beneath its crusty surface the ground was soft and yielding. The fields surrounding the graveyard were baked solid by the summer sun, yet this earth seemed to have been turned over recently.

"Moles?" Robert suggested, guessing what she was thinking.

"Maybe. Probably rabbits though, or hares. I heard my father say only the other day that the fields around here were infested with rabbits."

On hands and knees, Robert peered into the widening hole. "I hope my watch hasn't fallen into some rabbit warren."

Karen laughed at a sudden Alice-in-Wonderland image of a rabbit running around wearing Robert's watch.

"I see something," Robert said suddenly.

Karen stopped digging. "Did you bring a torch?"

"All I brought," he admitted, "was a couple of Mars bars."

"Maybe if we come across a rabbit, we can tempt it with your Mars bar," she replied sarcastically. "Go back to my bike and lift off the front lamp."

"Brilliant idea!" he said, darting off.

Karen concentrated on enlarging the hole. She soon discovered that she was working at one end of a deep, rectangular depression in the earth. The edge closest to the path had crumbled away, leaving the earth broken, looking almost as if it had been dug up and then deliberately and carefully replaced. As she cleared away more and more of the earth, she observed that the ground was pitted with a series of deep holes. Maybe Robert's watch had slid down one of the holes.

"The batteries aren't very strong," said Robert as he returned with the bicycle lamp, shining it on the palm of his hand.

"Well, there's no need to waste them any more," the girl retorted. She snatched the lamp from his hand and shone it down into the hole. "I see it!" she cried moments later. "Or at least I see something." She drew back and allowed Robert to stare down. At the end of a long, almost circular hole in the ground, light glinted off metal far below.

"It looks like it," he said, relieved that he had discovered his watch, dismayed because it was so far down. "But how are we going to get it out, Karen?"

Grinning, she tossed him the small gardening fork. "Dig."

"Hope no one sees us," Robert muttered. "They'll think we're grave robbers."

Fifteen minutes later, they had enlarged the hole enough for them to see Robert's watch clearly in the circle of pale yellow light cast by Karen's lamp. The watch was lying in the centre of what looked like a square stone box.

"Looks like it's lying on a pipe," said the boy . He rolled up his sleeve and lay flat on the ground with his cheek against the earth and his arm reaching as far down as it would go. "Sewers, maybe. Though I didn't think there were any sewers running under the old church." His fingers touched stone, slimy and cold, then brushed across something that felt hairy – which he desperately hoped was a root and not what he thought it was – and finally touched the glass face of his watch. "Got it!" he cried triumphantly.

At that moment Karen screamed.

CHAPTER NINE

"I'm fine. I'm fine," Karen insisted. She was leaning against the stone wall, arms folded tightly across her chest, Robert's jumper thrown over her shoulders. Beneath the thin, damp cloth of her tee-shirt she could feel her heart tripping madly, and her stomach was fluttering so wildly that she knew if she moved, she was going to be sick.

"Look, I think I should go and get some help," suggested Robert. He sounded worried. Karen's face was the colour of old paper, and although it wasn't particularly warm, he could see the sweat shining on her forehead.

"I'm fine," she insisted in an irritable voice. "It's my own fault," she added more gently, "I came out this morning without any breakfast, that's all."

"You never have any breakfast . . . " Robert began.

"Then I cycled like a mad thing to get down here. I was also bent over digging. I've just got a headache and a sick stomach."

"But . . . but why did you scream?" Robert asked. "You scared the . . . "

"I saw a spider," she snapped. "You know I don't like spiders."

Robert shook his head; it was the first time he'd heard her say any such thing. "Was it a very big spider?"

"As big as your head. Hairier too," she added, trying to make light of the event. "Look, why don't you go and get your watch? We can head back together."

"Will you be all right?" he asked anxiously.

"I'll be fine."

Karen waited until Robert had walked around behind the tower before abandoning the support of the stone wall and hurrying away from the vicinity of the church. Obviously Robert couldn't feel it, but there was a frightening aura of coldness clinging to the place.

She wasn't sure what had happened earlier. One moment she'd been watching Robert lying on the ground reaching down the hole, and then . . . and then . . . and then she felt as if a great dark cloud was rolling over her, filling her nose and mouth, clogging her ears, smothering her. The world went dark and for an instant she couldn't breathe. With her last breath, she screamed. The sound had shocked even her.

When Robert returned, Karen was sitting on the ground some distance from the ruined church with her back against a low hedge. Her eyes were closed, her face turned towards the sun. He was relieved to see that some colour had returned to her cheeks and the waxy pallor had vanished from her skin. Crouching beside her, deliberately holding his head so that its shadow fell across her face, he waited until she opened her eyes and squinted up at him. Then he held up the watch. "Got it!"

Karen reached out and lifted the watch from his fingers, brushing dirt from the leather strap. "Is it still running?"

"Absolutely," Robert said confidently. "Waterproof, shockproof . . . "

"Looks like just another watch to me."

"It cost one hundred and twenty pounds."

"One hundred and twenty pounds!" The girl ran her fingers over the metal back of the watch case. She wasn't going to tell Robert that it looked like a Swatch Watch. "What's it made out of – solid platinum?"

"Silver, actually."

After Karen passed the watch back to Robert, she rubbed her fingertips together. Her fingers were tingling, the pads feeling numb and slightly swollen. Checking the ground around her in case she had sat close to a nettle or some poison ivy, she got to her feet.

"What are you doing?" she asked abruptly, unable to conceal the exasperation in her voice.

Robert looked at her in surprise. "Putting my watch on."

"So you can lose it again? Put it in your pocket until you can get the strap fixed. You can be so stupid sometimes," she added, picking up her bike and pushing it through the gap in the hedge on to the narrow country road.

Robert stared after the girl, about to respond, but he bit back his answer. She was right, of course – putting the watch back on to his wrist before it was repaired was a stupid thing to do – but normally Karen would have made a bit of a joke about it. This time she sounded serious. She obviously wasn't well this morning. He hoped she wasn't coming down with flu; they'd planned to go to the disco on Friday night.

Robert pushed his bike through the hedge, expecting to find Karen waiting for him on the other side. Instead, he was surprised to discover that she had ridden off down the road. "Hey, wait for me!" he called.

The girl didn't even look back.

Standing under the shower, Karen tilted her face to the water and closed her eyes and mouth, then she drew her fingers through her long hair, pulling it back off her face. The warm water felt good against her cool skin, the steam and pressure of the needle spray against her shoulders easing taut muscles. She worked her head from side to side, trying to ease the pressure on the base of her neck; she felt as if there was a red-hot bar along the length of her spine.

Reaching up, she massaged the back of her neck with both hands, then hissed with pain as her left hand touched a very sore scratch on the side of her neck. When she looked at her fingers she was shocked to discover that they were slick with blood. More blood was running in a crimson thread down the length of her arm, spattering on to the floor of the shower stall where it was swirled away by the water.

Karen gasped in surprise. Pressing her hand against the cut, she pushed open the door and dashed across to the mirror. From the amount of blood she had seen in the shower, she expected to find quantities of blood pouring from the torn wound, covering her neck and hand. But the puncture marks on her neck were barely visible holes, tiny pink indentations in her skin, the scratches from the comb's teeth faded to pale, almost invisible lines.

There was no blood.

The girl stared into the mirror with wide, frightened eyes. "What is happening to me?" she asked. Her voice, sounding muffled and flat, was lost in the silence of the room.

"I think she's coming down with a cold, Robert," Catherine O'Sullivan said, stepping out into the early afternoon sunshine and pulling the door closed behind her to prevent Byte, the German Shepherd pup, from making an escape. It had taken them four hours to find her the last time she ran away, and then another two hours of scrubbing to clean the straw and horse manure off her.

"I thought she'd be out for the day with you," Catherine added, shading her eyes with her hand. Looking up at her, Robert could see how Karen would look in thirty years' time; they both had the same strong cheekbones, the same high forehead.

"She looked very pale this morning," he said.

"She's been in bed all afternoon. Whenever I looked in on her she's been dozing, though I heard the radio earlier, one of those chat shows. However, when I last brought her in a cup of tea she'd turned the radio off and gone back to sleep."

"Well, tell her I called." Robert picked up his bike from against the wall and reluctantly headed it toward home.

"She'll probably ring you later," Karen's mother told him. She stepped back inside the hall and pulled the door closed. Robert could hear Byte's high-pitched yapping as he pushed his bike down the path. Stopping at the gate, he turned back towards the cottage, looking toward the windows of Karen's room.

The curtains were drawn, but even as he watched he saw them twitch. Then they were pinched together in the centre as if someone had been looking out and was now holding them closed.

Puzzled, Robert propped his bike against the wall and darted back down along the path, hoping that Mrs O'Sullivan wasn't watching. Any explanation might be difficult. Crouching low, he scurried around the side of the house, then straightened outside Karen's window. There he pressed himself against the glass and stared in through the crack between the curtains.

For a moment he could see nothing. Then, as his eyes adjusted to the gloom, he started to make out shapes: the bedside lockers, the clock radio, the time – six-eighteen – winking in red digits, and the bed. The sheet was thrown back and the bed was empty.

He started to smile; Karen was probably hiding on the other side of the curtains watching *him*. Any moment now she was going to pull back the curtains and attempt to startle him. Well, he was going to disappoint her, he was going to stand here and not move a muscle . . .

Just then he caught sight of Karen sitting before the dressing table.

Puzzled, he moved to one side so he could look into the room at an angle and see her more clearly. She was wearing the *Love Is* pyjamas he had given her for her birthday, and slowly and methodically combing her hair. He rapped gently on the window, but the girl didn't move. Pressing his nose to the glass, Robert cupped his hands around his eyes and stared in.

That was when he realised that Karen was combing her hair with her eyes closed. She was still asleep.

CHAPTER TEN

The castle was always cold, even on the warmest summer days. The old stones never warmed up, and the narrow slit windows funnelled an icy chill into the room.

The girl sitting before the polished metal mirror was combing her hair. She gazed at her distorted reflection, noting the paleness of her skin, the touch of blue around her lips. She could not feel the chill – it had been a long time since she had experienced any physical sensations – but she knew that her flesh was cold to the touch. She was also aware that the air around her was icy, and was conscious that one of the coldest winters in living memory gripped the land.

Closing her eyes, she sighed. She was cold, so cold, but it was not hot air, or a warm fire or a furred cloak that could warm her.

Opening her eyes, she stared into the mirror . . . and for an instant, a single instant, saw another face in the metal, a face like, yet unlike, her own. It appeared against a background both strange and bizarre. Resting her pointed chin on her hand, she studied the image. It was that of a girl roughly her own age.

Then she began to laugh. Unless the girl was one of the Sith, there was no possible way that they were of an age. She had been a child when Nebuchadnezzar ruled Babylon nearly six hundred years before the coming of the man known as the White Christ. And this was now the Year of Our Lord, 1420 . . . so that made her more than two thousand years old.

Two thousand years, compared to the youthful features of the child in the mirror!

When the young women threw back her head, her laughter sounded like a beast's howling. In her distorted reflection in the metal mirror, her teeth looked unnaturally long.

And as she laughed, the other figure in the mirror, that of a blond girl combing her hair, twitched in an uneasy sleep.

CHAPTER ELEVEN

Patrick Ellis crouched on the rock with a can of foaming lager clutched between his knees. Weighing the stone carefully in his hand, he suddenly launched it at the plastic bottle bobbing on the waves almost directly in front of him. He made a small explosive sound with his mouth as the stone scored a direct hit, the force of the blow momentarily dipping the bottle below the surface. When the waves carried the battered bottle out on the tide, he rewarded himself with a swig from the can, coughing as the tart liquid burned at the back of his throat.

Glancing down, he checked that the remainder of the six pack was still nestling in the shade of the rocks, staying cool. Turning his hand palm up, he glanced at the watch on the studded black leather band on his wrist and frowned; the others were late.

There were advantages to living in Skerries, Patrick knew: clean air, and clean beaches. But the disadvantages outweighed them as far as he could see. There was nothing to do at night. The town was nearly twenty miles from Dublin, and served by an irregular bus and train service. So, going into the city to the cinema or a gig meant leaving early to catch the last bus or train home . . .

and if you missed it, there was nothing else to do but to try and hitch a lift. And if you were six foot one with a green-tipped Mohican haircut, wearing slashed jeans and a battered leather jacket at least three sizes too large, there was very little chance of getting a lift from any car that didn't have a revolving blue light on top of it.

There were plenty of pubs in Skerries, but Patrick and his friends – most of whom were underage anyway – had managed to get themselves barred from all of them. There was no cinema, and they'd been barred from the amusement arcade at the far end of the seafront for wrecking one of the slot machines. Patrick grinned at the memory. Marty Bateman had poured coke into one of the slot machines, thinking that he could short circuit it into delivering a jackpot. The machine had shorted in a spectacular shower of sparks and plunged the whole building into darkness.

Just as he was reliving the memory, somewhere in the distance a motorbike rumbled. Patrick turned his head, following the sound, identifying the bike by the particular rumble of the engines: 500cc Kawasaki.

That's what he needed. A motor bike. If he had a bike he'd be free to come and go as he pleased. He sipped more of the lager, smiling at the thought. He'd no longer be dependent on buses or trains; it would take him thirty minutes to get into the city. He'd have a great excuse to get all the proper leather gear: the jacket, leather trousers and high boots. He ran his hand across the bristling top of his lacquered hair. He wasn't sure what he'd do with his hair, though . . . maybe they made special motorcycle helmets for punk hairstyles?

He laughed aloud at the bizarre image. Finishing the last of the can, he attempted to crumple it in his fist, but failed. Dropping it on the stones, he stamped on it, then picked up the can and placed it by his side. The others could think that he'd crushed it by hand.

Patrick looked at his watch again. Where were they? Reaching down, he pulled out another can and snapped the top back, swearing softly as foam cascaded over his hand, soaking into his sleeve.

Should he have a bike . . . or a car?

Maybe a car would be better. A two seater . . . no, a four seater, he could take his friends into the gigs with him, and a car would impress the girls. But there was no way his father would pay for a car . . .

A shadow fell across him and he turned too quickly, drunk enough to be unsteady. "Well it's about time . . ." he began, then stopped.

It wasn't whom he'd been expecting.

CHAPTER TWELVE

Robert moved slowly around Karen's bedroom, tilting his head to one side to read the paperback titles in the bookcase. He recognised none of the authors. "How do you feel?" he asked, glancing over his shoulder.

"Better," Karen replied slowly.

"You don't sound so sure," he said with a laugh.

She raised her voice to sound more confident. "I feel much better, really." Sitting up in the bed, she drew her knees up to her chin and wrapped her arms around her legs.

"You look a lot better," he told her, standing at the foot of the bed, suddenly – unaccountably – feeling shy in her presence. "Yesterday, you looked . . . really ill."

Karen grinned. "Why, Robert Carroll, you sound almost as if you care."

"I was worried," he admitted, then added quickly, "if you were too sick to go to the disco on the beach on Friday night, I'd have had to find someone else to go with."

"Who?" she asked sharply.

"Probably Jean Elliott," he said with a sly smile, knowing Karen detested the girl.

Karen flung a pillow at Robert just as the door to her room opened and her mother appeared, carrying a tray. The pillow struck the wall beside her, almost knocking over the pitcher of orange juice. "I thought I told you no messing," Catherine O'Sullivan said with a frown. She put down the tray on the bedside locker and lifted a thermometer. Shaking it hard, she popped it into Karen's mouth.

"I was just saying she's looking much better today," Robert remarked.

"Yes. I think it was just one of those twenty-four hour bugs. We caught it in time. How do you feel?" she asked her daughter.

Karen's reply was an indecipherable mumble because the thermometer was still in her mouth. Her mother removed the thin glass cylinder, turning it to check the temperature.

"It's normal," she reported, sounding relieved.

"Does that mean I can get up?" Karen asked hopefully.

"I suppose so."

"Can I go out?"

"No. You can stay inside today and shake off that bug. You can go out tomorrow."

Karen was about to argue, but she could tell by the expression on her mother's face that she wouldn't win. "When can I get up, then?"

"After lunch," Catherine said, leaving the room. She paused at the door and looked back at Robert. "Are you staying for lunch?"

"No thanks, Mrs O'Sullivan, I'll head home and come back later."

"Don't stay too long then; let Karen get some rest."

"I'm fine . . ." the girl began, but the door had already closed behind her mother. "She worries too much," said Karen. She nodded at the orange juice. "Pour us a drink, that looks good."

Robert poured two glasses of freshly squeezed orange juice, easing pips out of the glass with his thumb. "I called yesterday," he said casually, watching Karen's reflection in the mirror.

"Mum told me."

"As I was leaving I thought I saw the curtains move." He smiled as he carried the glasses back over to the bed. "I thought you might have been watching me."

Karen shook her head. "I didn't hear the door. I must have been asleep." She rolled the sweating glass between the palms of her hands and stared down into the orange liquid. In truth, she couldn't remember much about yesterday; her last really clear memory was of helping Robert dig out his watch. After that everything went a bit . . . strange. When she'd finally awakened shortly after dawn, she'd lain in her bed for several long moments wondering where she was and how she had got there.

She glanced up to find Robert watching her closely. "What?" she asked.

"Nothing," he smiled. He raised his glass in salute. "Drink up."

Karen brought the glass to her lips and tilted her head back. As the liquid flowed down the glass towards her mouth, tendrils of red swirled through it. The girl drew back her head with a start.

"What's wrong?" Robert wanted to know.

"Nothing . . . nothing," she said shakily. "I thought I saw something in the glass." Karen tilted the glass from side to side. Strips of pulp and peel floated in the juice.

"Probably a pip." Robert finished his drink in one quick swallow. "Anyway, I'm off . . ."

"What are you going to do today?"

"There is a film crew setting up in the grounds of Ardgillan Castle. Apparently they're using the house to shoot some historical drama, something about the Famine. I thought I'd cycle up there to see what's happening. Maybe they'll offer me a part," he added. "I might be *discovered*."

"You'll be discovered all right . . . as an idiot," she laughed.

"You can laugh . . ."

"Thanks, I will."

". . . but you'll be laughing on the other side of your face when I'm a famous movie star like Arnold Schwarzenegger."

Karen started laughing. Robert was the skinniest boy she knew.

"Well, maybe not Arnold Schwarzenegger," Robert said ruefully, flexing non-existent muscles. "How about Jean Claude Van Damme . . . he's slim . . . or Brad Pitt," he said, naming Karen's favourite star of the moment. "He's not muscular."

"You haven't got the hair to be a Brad Pitt," she laughed.

Robert's expression sobered. "It's good to see you laughing again," he told her. "You had me worried yesterday." He was about to say more, but suddenly turned away. "See you later." He left the room before she could see the spots of colour burning on his cheeks.

Karen climbed out of bed and crossed to the window. Pulling back the curtains, she watched Robert lift his bike from against the wall, then turn and wave. She waved back, then stood at the window, watching him until he vanished around the bend in the road. She was vaguely disappointed that he didn't look back before he disappeared.

Turning back to the bedside locker, she lifted the glass of orange juice, holding it up to the light, swirling the liquid, looking for the red she had glimpsed moments earlier. There was nothing. Just ordinary juice, sweet and cold. She drank quickly, flavour flooding her mouth . . . and instantly turning foul: hot and salt and meaty. She barely made it to the sink before she threw up.

CHAPTER THIRTEEN

Ardgillan Castle had never been a real castle. It was a large impressive manor house, which had been built in 1738 and then been added to over the years until it was now a mixture of styles. At some stage castellations had been added in an attempt to make the roof look like a castle wall. From the sloping front lawn, it was possible to look out across Skerries to the right. If the weather was reasonably clear, one could see the blue shoulders of the Mountains of Mourne to the north, across an expanse of sea.

The landscaped grounds had been opened to the public in 1986, and although cycling in the park was expressly forbidden, Robert often sneaked his mountain bike into the grounds to ride, dangerously fast, on the narrow winding walks.

The park was usually deserted during the week, though on Saturdays or Sundays, if the weather was fine, it would attract a crowd, but it was just a little too far out from the city, and just a little too far off the beaten track to be really popular.

Today, however, it was crowded.

Robert slowed as he came down the long narrow road

that led directly into the main gates of the castle. There were people everywhere, cars parked in a solid line along the soft margins, making the already narrow road almost impassable. A white police car, lights slowly revolving, was parked across the entrance gate to the left, while the right hand gate, the exit, was closed. People in 17th century costume were milling around just inside the gates, drinking water from plastic bottles, while in the distance, tall arc lights blazed over the tree tops, even though the sky was cloudless.

Robert manoeuvred his way through the people, using his bike as a shield to push himself to the front of the crowd. Most of the faces he recognised; they were locals from Skerries, some from Balbriggan or Loughshinny. "What's happening?" he asked no one in particular.

"They've closed off the park," an old man said indignantly. "And it's supposed to be a public park," he added with obvious resentment.

The police officer standing before the gate ignored him.

"I walk here every day," a woman added. "They have no right to do this."

"So do I come here," a man in a tracksuit said, "to jog. I have the distance all measured out. What am I going to do now?"

"It's only for a couple of days," the police officer explained, finally forced to acknowledge the crowd. He jerked his thumb over his shoulder. "Think of all the money they're spending locally."

"Nothing," a woman said bitterly. "I've a shop down in Skerries and I can tell you that they're spending nothing.

Every bit of their food is brought in to them in those huge catering vans, and when they've finished work for the day, they all go back into the city."

"Maybe you'll get some work on the film," suggested the officer, folding his arms and leaning back against the patrol car.

"They haven't hired a single person from around here," the woman continued. "This is our park, and I personally feel that . . ."

Robert had heard enough. He pushed his way out of the crowd, then hopped on his bike and freewheeled down the hill towards the sea, brakes squealing as he tried to prevent himself building up too much speed. Insects batted against his face and he kept his mouth tightly shut; he had once swallowed a fly while cycling and the sudden shock and disgust had sent him tumbling off the bike. The fall cost him a broken left wrist but taught him a valuable lesson.

He slowed as he came to the foot of the steep hill, braking sharply as he sped past the stables on the left, back wheel locking, skidding, the horses in their stalls following the screech of his tyres with bright eyes and twitching ears. He pedalled under a stone railway bridge, the air momentarily chill, then turned to the left on to the main road. To his right the sea was a brilliant blue, the water looking almost metallic, with swirls of deeper green indicating the currents, and tiny flecks of white foam marking the positions of half-submerged rocks.

Robert often cycled down on to the beach to hunt for fossils along the cliff face – usually with Karen. He'd spent a lot of time with her this summer. They frequently walked on the beach together, supposedly looking for fossils, but most of the time they simply strolled along the sand and stones, talking, always talking. They never seemed to run out of things to say to each other.

Robert smiled tightly when he realised that he could feel colour in his cheeks. When his family had taken the house in Skerries for the summer he'd been dead set against it, because he'd have to leave Susanne, his girlfriend. They'd promised to write every day, but he'd got only one letter from her, though he'd written three times.

He was beginning to realise now that he'd never had the feelings for Susanne that he had for Karen.

The metal footbridge that crossed the railway lines and the adjacent road had been built in the middle of the nineteenth century by the railway company, when the Taylor family, who owned Ardgillan, had allowed the railway track to cut through a portion of their property. The footbridge gave access to a small private beach, where the remains of the Taylors' private bathing shelter was slowly crumbling into the sea. Known locally as the Ladies' Stairs, the place supposedly got its name because it was supposed to be haunted by a ghostly lady. But Robert reckoned it was called that because it had been used by the ladies of the house.

As the boy cycled under the narrow metal bridge, he saw that the spiked metal gate at one end was swinging open. Shouldering his heavy mountain bike, he started up the concrete stairs leading to the gate. He had expected the gate on the Ladies' Stairs to be open; it usually was. Only the local people would be aware of its existence, however.

Whenever he wanted to sneak his bike into the grounds of Ardgillan, this was the route he used. He paused on the bridge for a few moments, looking down on to the railway track, hoping he would see a train in the distance. It was an exhilarating experience to be standing on the metal bridge while a train thundered past a few feet below, making the iron structure hum and tremble. If the train driver saw him, he would sound the whistle and wave.

But there were no trains in sight. Robert wondered if they were delayed or rescheduled because of the filming. Might sound a bit odd if a modern train was heard rushing by in what was supposed to be the 17th century.

Crossing the bridge, he started down, allowing his bike to bump its way on the steps. At the foot of the stairs he stepped into tree-shaded gloom. Leaves and twigs crackled underfoot as he moved off down a narrow dirt track, where the trees crowded so closely together they formed a tunnel. Breathing deeply, filling his lungs with the slightly cloying, earthy odour of vegetation, Robert was suddenly aware of the absolute silence that surrounded him. Usually Ardgillan was alive with birdsong, while the undergrowth rustled with the unseen movement of rabbits, hares and foxes. But nothing moved today, no birds sang in the trees; the air was thick and still.

The film crew must have startled them . . .

Suddenly Robert had the unmistakable feeling that he was being watched.

He continued walking. Should he turn, or run?

With every step he took the feeling grew stronger. A cold prickling swept across his shoulders.

It was probably just one of the park keepers, he told

himself. No doubt they were watching the bridge, expecting someone to try to sneak on to the movie set. He should have known better . . .

He could hop on his bike, pedal away furiously; there was no way a park keeper would be able to catch him – unless they had radios. Had they radios? Surely they did.

Maybe it would be better if he turned back; the keeper might just let him go.

Taking a deep breath, Robert pasted an apologetic smile on his face and turned around . . .

CHAPTER FOURTEEN

Karen splashed cold water on her face, but it did not help much. Her skin was clammy and hot and there was an ugly fluttering in the pit of her stomach. She was sure she was going to be sick again in a minute. Leaning straight arms on the edges of the sink, she stared into the water-speckled mirror. What was happening to her?

Her skin was ghastly white, her eyes reddened with a number of tiny burst blood vessels. Her cheeks were hollow and her lips were cracked and dry. She seemed to have aged years in a matter of hours.

Bracing herself, Karen raised a trembling hand to her forehead.

The figure in the mirror did not mimic her movement.

Slowly, trying not to panic, Karen lowered her eyes to the sink. Ignoring the mirror, she turned the cold tap, watching the liquid swirl down the plughole before cupping her hand and filling her palm with water. Bending close to the sink, she splashed her face and then ran a wet hand across the back of her neck to cool herself further.

She was hallucinating . . . that was it . . . she was hallucinating.

There was something wrong with the water.

The realisation took hold slowly. She had been staring down without really seeing anything, but there was something *wrong* about the liquid in the basin, something very strange . . .

It was curling down the plughole in an anti-clockwise direction!

Karen felt her stomach heave again. Was this another hallucination? Well if it was, it was curious rather than frightening. North of the equator, water spun in a clockwise direction; south of the equator, it spun counter-clockwise. They learned that in school.

She turned the tap, slowing the water to a trickle . . . but it still revolved anti-clockwise before it disappeared down the plughole.

She held her fingers under the tap. The thread of water was cool and very wet, a most realistic hallucination . . .

Raising her head, she looked into the mirror again. She was looking at her reflection . . . but here too there was something wrong, something out of place. Her reflection wasn't sharply defined, the edges were blurred. She reached out to swipe mist from the glass . . . and once again the reflection in the mirror didn't mimic her movement.

Karen's teeth began to chatter. She was seeing things because she was feverish . . . she would go back to bed, and get her mother to call the doctor.

But as the girl was turning away from the mirror, she saw Robert in the glass. The image was so clear and distinct she could identify where he was. He was standing on the earthen track in Ardgillan close to the foot of the Ladies' Stairs. He was pushing his bike, walking away from her . . . then he slowed . . . and turned toward her, with a smile on his face.

Automatically, Karen smiled back, only to see the boy's face twist into a mask of disgust and horror. She could not hear anything, but she saw him open his mouth and scream.

In the hallway outside her door, Byte, the German Shepherd pup, began howling.

CHAPTER FIFTEEN

Her people did not die.

Her people, the Sith, had been old before the first of the apes had climbed down from the trees. Her people had nurtured the fledgling race, encouraged them, taught them their first lessons, shown them how to farm and work stone and soft metals. Her people had instructed the first humans in the mystery of fire, given them a language and learning.

It was not easy. The first humans remained primitive and ape-like; they were brutal, cannibal savages who killed often and without need, who slaughtered whole herds of beasts for a single meal . . . and who sometimes turned against their masters.

But the humans had one great weakness, one terrible fear. They were short-lived and so they feared death. The Sith were long-lived and death was virtually unknown among them. Twenty summers was old for the first humans; twenty centuries of life was commonplace for the Sith.

Even as the human race evolved and multiplied, and their quality of life improved, forty or sometimes fifty summers was considered a great age. Men and women who survived for seventy summers were considered ancient and venerated for the wisdom they had accumulated in their long lives. The Sith took time to instruct these elders, seeding them with knowledge they could pass on to their tribes . . . but little realising that they were planting the seeds of their own destruction.

Soon those of the human-kind who lived long began to notice that the Sith did not age . . . nor did they eat nor drink in the manner of humans.

The stories began then, scraps of whispered tales and fragments of half truths. Once the stories had begun, they could not be stopped. They grew and grew with each telling, making the Sith monsters, weaving around them a terrifying legend. The humans, who had once worshipped the Sith as gods, now came to fear and loathe them. One by one the great Sith families were driven out. Those who didn't flee were hunted down and destroyed by the frightened humans.

It did not happen overnight. It took, perhaps, a thousand years, for the Sith to completely withdraw from the World of Men. In some places, the high mountains, the hidden valleys, the isolated hamlets, the Sith remained in their accustomed positions of authority, retaining human subjects who remained loyal. They kept these humans well-fed and well-sheltered, and in return, the Sith took *tribute*.

But these situations were far too few. In human eyes, the Sith had become monsters to be hunted down and destroyed. Little did the humans realise that they were destroying their own future.

If the Sith had remained among the human kind, they

could have given them science and technology beyond their ability to imagine. By now, in the last few years of the period known as the twentieth century, humans should have colonised the planets in the Solar System and started the great push out into space. But they had thrown all that aside when they turned against the Sith.

And simply because the Sith occasionally fed off the flesh and blood of the humans.

What was so wrong with that? The humans fed off other beasts, including animals they raised for that specific purpose. So too had the Sith fed off the humans and farmed them.

The early human kind had feared so many, many things. As they had become more and more civilised, they lost some of the old fears and learned new ones. But the deepest terrors stayed with them; they always feared the night, and the creatures that lurked in the shadows.

And they especially feared the Sith.

Over the eons human language changed. Consonants and vowels took on different sounds. Eventually Sith became *Seech* and *Veech* and *Leach* and *Leech*, and *Leech* became *Litch*, and Litch became *amptch* and *ampyre* – and this in time became Vampyre.

But although the name changed, the meaning remained the same: blood drinker.

In time the vampyre became merely a legend, nothing more than a colourful horror story.

But not forgotten.

And in their secret hearts humans continued to fear the vampyre . . . because deep down, they knew that this was no story. They knew that the legend was real.

Now the few vampyre who had survived the centuries of persecution slept in their sunless chambers, while years rolled into centuries in the World of Men. All they needed was blood to bring them awake.

The red-haired vampyre smiled and licked her full lips. She was awake now. Alert and alive, conscious of the stone coffin surrounding her, the weight of earth and stones above her, conscious too of the scents of life seeping into the coffin. All she needed was a little more blood to restore her to her full power.

But even though her body was trapped, her spirit wandered free. She sought out the girl who was linked to her, the girl whose soul she had touched, whose dreams she had invaded. Closing her eyes, she found herself looking at the blond girl . . . and the girl was seeing a boy framed by trees.

The vampyre looked at the boy.

And he looked back.

CHAPTER SIXTEEN

"A trick of the light . . . nothing more than a trick of the light." Robert Carroll breathed deeply, leaning on the low stone wall, looking down over the broad stretch of beach below.

Turning his head to the left, he glanced up at the metal bridge, following it with his eyes until it disappeared among the trees in Ardgillan's wooded parkland. He had no conscious memory of grabbing his bike and racing up the stairs and across the bridge. All he could remember was the face . . .

The face in the trees.

He attempted a smile; even now it sounded ludicrous. Then his smile faded. The vision had seemed so real . . .

When he had turned around, he had been expecting to see a park-keeper, or maybe even the movie company's security people standing behind him. But the track was deserted.

And yet he had known someone was there. The feeling of being watched persisted and intensified. He knew, without any shadow of a doubt, that someone was watching him. The weight of eyes lay heavy upon him.

He made himself stare into the deepest shadows, where

the green gloom faded to impenetrability. But he could see nothing. The leaves, rustling and whispering in the breeze, seemed to mock him, whispering secrets.

He was turning away when he realised that there was no breeze. The afternoon was still and calm.

Not really frightened yet, but intrigued and intensely curious, Robert stepped closer to the trees. He craned his head to squint up into the gloom. Sunlight filtering through green leaves blinked down at him.

Except that it wasn't sunlight.

Eyes. Cold, green eyes. Staring at him, wide and unblinking.

The huge black pupils contracted, narrowed, slitted. And then the teeth appeared.

He screamed aloud, but the crouching trees swallowed the sound.

Robert grabbed his bike, turned and ran.

He felt foolish now. With a final look over his shoulder, he set off down the coast road, pedalling slowly, the long muscles in his thighs still trembling from shock. Thinking back on the incident, he assured himself he had probably seen an owl. A barn owl or a grey owl. The bird must have been sleeping in the trees and he'd disturbed it. He'd tell Karen about it later and she'd laugh; it would be good to see her laugh.

Well, so much for his chances to see a movie being made. He had been frightened away not by the park keepers or movie security, but an owl.

Robert was still smiling sheepishly to himself as he rounded the corner and noticed the white police car ahead.

It was angled in against the road, blue light revolving slowly, the colour pale and wan in the strong daylight. A small crowd had gathered around the car. More people were leaning against the low sea wall, staring down on to the beach. In the distance an ambulance siren wailed.

Even before he hopped off the bike, Robert knew what to expect. Someone had injured themselves on the rocks below. It happened every summer. This end of the beach was wild and rocky, slippery with green slime and seaweed. The lure of the boulders was irresistible and people – usually young men and boys – insisted on clambering over them. It was very easy to slip, to trap an ankle and snap it. Robert had known a couple of cases where people had been knocked out when they'd fallen and struck their heads on the jagged stones.

He saw Peter Kater standing in the crowd and manoeuvred his way through to stand beside the short, blond-haired boy. Peter sat three seats behind him in class. They nodded to one another. "What's up?" Robert asked.

Peter pulled off his wire framed glasses and wiped them on his *Babylon* 5 T-shirt. "A body on the beach," he replied, fighting hard not to stammer. "I think it's dead."

Robert leaned over the wall to stare down on to the rocks and shingle. A single police officer, two local men and a man he recognised as Doctor Elliott were crouched beside an untidy bundle of seaweed-covered rags wedged between the stones. The bundle was hardly recognisable, but when Robert stared hard enough he knew it was human. "Drowned?" he asked Peter.

"Don't know."

"Anyone we know?"

Peter didn't answer, merely nudged Robert in the ribs and nodded to where a tall, hard-faced woman was standing on the beach, a little apart from the others. Her wringing hands were slowly shredding a tissue to confetti. Robert frowned. "That looks like Mrs Ellis, Paddy's mother . . ." he began, and then stopped as the realisation struck home.

He turned to look at the body on the beach again, squinting to make out the shape. Finally, he distinguished faded blue jeans, and a single wine-coloured Doc Marten boot at the end of a twisted leg. The other foot, entwined in seaweed, was bare.

Paddy Ellis?

It couldn't be. He'd seen Paddy Ellis only yesterday, green-tinged Mohican haircut bobbing as he rode his mountain bike over the low sand dunes.

"I was to meet him last night," Peter Kater said softly. "Me and a few of the lads. Drink a few cans, smoke a couple of fags." The boy's voice was tight and he kept swallowing hard. "When we got to the beach he wasn't there. But there was blood on the sand. Spots of blood. They were still wet." Tears welled in his eyes and rolled slowly down his cheeks. "This wasn't an accident."

Robert rubbed his fingers across dry lips. "Of course it was an accident," he said reassuringly. "Maybe Paddy had too much to drink . . . went for a swim and got into difficulties."

"He's still wearing his clothes," Peter replied hoarsely. He turned and began pushing his way through the growing crowd. "This wasn't an accident," he repeated over his shoulder.

Robert followed the other boy until they were well away from the onlookers. When he was sure they were out of earshot he said quietly. "You saw something, didn't you?"

Even before Peter started to shake his head, Robert knew he was lying.

"I didn't see anything."

"What was it? What did you see?" Robert demanded. He manoeuvred his bike in front of Peter, forcing him to a halt. "Tell me."

The younger boy looked away.

"You were there, weren't you?" Robert guessed.

Peter nodded without looking at him. "I saw someone on the beach," he finally admitted.

"Someone? Who?"

When Peter looked up his eyes were dark and accusing, then he turned his head so that he would not have to look at Robert as he spoke.

"Karen O'Sullivan."

"Impossible!"

"It was Karen," Peter said firmly. "She was talking to Paddy, then they turned and went down behind the sand-dunes."

Robert was still shaking his head, but Peter pressed on. "I crept up behind the dunes. I was going to surprise them, frighten them . . . but when I got there they had both vanished. That's when I discovered the blood," he whispered.

CHAPTER SEVENTEEN

Dreams.

That was the great power of the Sith. They knew the power of dreams, knew how to use and interpret what they called the Sleeping World, or the Dreamscape. To them, the Dreamscape was as real and as vivid as the physical world. Unlike the Race of Man, which separated the two existences, condemning one as a figment of the imagination, the Sith embraced the Dreamscape and learned how to utilise it.

In Sith legend, there were many instances of one of the vampyre lying down and falling into a deep sleep from which they refused to awaken. When this happened, their families placed them in ornate wooden boxes and left them to sleep, knowing their loved ones were still living, but living in another existence. Knowing also that they would awaken days, weeks or months hence, at a time of their own choosing.

There were stories of those who had slept for tens of years, while others had slept for centuries. Some of these tales had been absorbed by the human kind into their mythology. But no one amongst the Sith had ever slept for nearly five hundred years.

Until . . . she did.

When the savage humans had buried her alive beneath the ground all those years ago they thought they had been condemning her to a brief agony until her life ultimately ran out. They did not understand the Sith biology. Deprived of light and air and fresh blood, the physical body had simply shut down, slipping into a deep hibernation. But though her body slept, her mind had remained conscious, and active.

The five hundred years she spent entombed beneath the earth had made her powerful. She had learned to shape and control the Dreamscape like no other of her kind; she had discovered how to move from her dream into the dreams of others, first as an observer, then as a participant, finally as a controller and dream-shaper.

But having lived for so long within her own imagination, within the world which she had created, she was finding it difficult to determine what was real and what still belonged to her Dreamscape.

Who was she now? She had had many names, in many tongues. In that place which history would call Assyria, she had been known as Ekimmu. In the city called Babylon which her people had raised from the desert, she had worn the name Lilitu. Some had called her Lamia. On the isle of Crete, she had been worshipped as Katalkanas; the Greeks took her name and made it Vrukalakos because of the colour of her hair. And when she lived in Rome, Gaius Julius Caesar had called her Strega.

Strega.

She was Strega. And that was the name she had chosen to carry down through the ages, when thinking of herself.

She had always loved Rome. She had lived there for many years, from the grand days of Caesar through the terrible days of Nero until the final days when the barbarians rode through the marbled streets.

Strega.

She had worn the name Vetch when she had come to the city on the Seven Hills and charmed the small, bald man who had conquered the known world. The Roman emperor had been unable to pronounce her name, so he had called her Strix. He softened this to Strega when he spoke to her of his campaigns in the dark forests of Gaul and the foggy land of the Britons. He spoke also of the mysterious Isle at the End of the World.

In the months that followed, the Romans, always keen to follow the latest fad, made Strega one of the most popular girl's names in the city. Women – and some men too – took to colouring their hair red to match hers.

But by the time she left Rome generations later, Strega was no longer being used as a girl's name. The word had become a curse.

She had wandered northwards in the forests Caesar had told her about. There she had found some of her own kind, the Sith, living as warlords, taking tribute from the local people. Moving eastward, she dwelled briefly with the Viesczy Sith, dark and powerful warriors who held the high mountain passes and exacted tribute in goods and blood from the travellers.

Then Strega had wandered northward, into the cold wet forests where she was known as Mara. Those were good times; the land was wild and lawless and few people paid attention to the apparently young woman who roamed through their settlements, stayed a night and moved on. There was little or no communication between the villages and so no one realised that wherever the red-haired girl went, there was always some terribly weakened person left behind.

If Strega had taken too much blood and her victim died, he or she would rise again – to feed off blood themselves. These undead were not true Sith, however, though in human folklore they became one and the same.

Strega moved westward next, following the route Caesar had taken centuries before. She explored the land of the Britons, staying at the court of Camlann with the savage warlord whom history would call Arthur. His chief advisor, Myrddyn, a mad old hedge wizard, had fallen deeply in love with her, though she detested him on sight. She also loathed the name he and Arthurus called her: Niniane.

In the stone coffin, tight skin moved as Strega smiled. In the end she had left Camlann before she was forced to kill Myrddyn. How would English history have fared then?

And finally she had come to the land of Erin, the Isle at the End of the World. Caesar had never visited Ireland. When he fought his British campaign he had been tired, his troops exhausted and his supplies stretched to the limits. The reputation of the Irish warriors and the dark magic of their druids was such that he did not wish to overstretch his resources.

Coming to Ireland proved to be the greatest mistake Strega would make in her overlong life.

The law of the White Christ was strong in this land; the

clans were closely knit and soon the finger of suspicion was pointed at the red-haired stranger. It took them nearly a hundred years to track her down, but when they did they put her into the ground.

Skin cracked, tiny slivers flaking away as her smile broadened. But had it been such a mistake? If she had remained on the European mainland she might have been betrayed like so many of her clan, destroyed outright or forced to spend her days in hiding.

When the savage Irish buried her, they had prayed over the tomb for some few years afterward, to keep her in her place. But the humans were short lived, and their memories even shorter. Soon they had forgotten who was buried in the ground; some believed that it was a holy woman, a saint. They built a chapel above the place where her body lay. Finally, even that story died out and Strega was forgotten, left to dream.

But now she was awake.

And the world had forgotten about her clan.

All she needed now was nourishment. With blood would come strength and power, and then nothing would stop her.

Opening her eyes wide, staring into the darkness, she allowed her mind to soar and touch the dreams of the girl. The girl who carried the comb.

CHAPTER EIGHTEEN

Catherine O'Sullivan was pulling the door closed behind her when Robert cycled up. The woman turned as she heard the gravel crunch, and even before she spoke Robert knew something was wrong.

"What's happened?" she demanded to know.

Robert was puzzled. Was she talking about the corpse that had been discovered earlier that afternoon? Surely all of Skerries knew about it by now. But before he could respond, the woman asked in an urgent tone, "Where's Karen?"

He looked at her blankly. "I don't know. I've just come down to see how she was."

"But didn't she go out to meet you just after tea?"

Robert shook his head.

"But she spoke to you on the phone this afternoon," Catherine O'Sullivan insisted. "I heard her making the call."

Robert was about to deny it; he hadn't spoke to Karen on the phone. But then he nodded slowly, unwilling to get the girl into trouble. "I forgot," he said lamely.

The woman turned the key in the door and walked over to the car. "I suppose you also forgot where you were meeting her?"

"I think we said we'd go down to the beach."

"She told me she was going to Baldungan Castle," Mrs O'Sullivan said, scowling. "She took Byte with her."

"Baldungan Castle," Rober hastily agreed. "Of course. I remember now."

"Although what you two would be doing there is quite beyond me."

"Research into the gravestones," the boy explained, thinking fast. The lie was growing. "A school project."

"That's what Karen said," Mrs O'Sullivan told him as she climbed into the three-year-old Volvo estate car. "She said you were working on some school project together." The tone of her voice made it perfectly clear that she didn't believe the story. "If that girl's not home soon, though . . ." But whatever the rest of the sentence was, Robert did not hear. It was lost in the roar of the engine as Karen's mother drove away.

It took him fifteen minutes to reach the castle; the journey usually took twenty-five. Red-faced and panting, he only slowed when he came in sight of the ruined castle and saw Karen's bike lying against the low stone wall that surrounded the graveyard. There was no sign of the girl, but she was probably on the other side of the ruin.

What was she doing here, Robert wondered. There was no school project, as he knew very well.

He cycled slowly down the dirt track that led from the road to the castle, standing on the pedals to give him extra height. But the entire area seemed deserted. The early evening air was calm, with just enough of a hint of breeze to take the heat off the day.

High above his head a single crow circled, cawing plaintively.

Placing his bike alongside Karen's, Robert hopped over the wall and followed it around to the left, into the chill shadow of the building, expecting to see the girl at any moment.

"Karen?" His voice echoed eerily through the ruin. He heard scrabbling from the opposite side of the building, stones rattling. "Karen?" he called again. The low evening sunlight caught him full in the eyes as he stepped through the archway of the ancient church. Blinking hard, with yellow and black spots burned on his retina, he heard the gravel crunch again.

He turned just as the creature – hair and teeth and foul breath – lunged up at him, sending him sprawling backwards, with not enough air left in his lungs to scream.

Robert opened his eyes as a wet, sticky tongue began licking his face from chin to eyebrows and slobbering over his forehead. "Byte." His voice was high-pitched and shaky. He took a deep breath, coughed and tried again. "Byte, stop it." Sitting up, he pushed the German Shepherd pup away from him and looked around, expecting to find Karen peering through the doorway, laughing at him.

But there was no sign of the girl.

CHAPTER NINETEEN

From where she was sitting, with her back against the gnarled trunk of an ancient oak tree, Karen could look down over the tumbled ruin of the church. She had never realised just how peaceful this place could be, how still and silent. It suddenly made her realise how noisy the world had become. It was never truly silent, there were always cars on the road, tyres squealing, engines rumbling, radios blaring and cackling, or people shouting, children crying, dogs barking . . . Once she had liked a lot of noise. But no more, she was discovering. Maybe she was growing up.

Here and now, it was still and silent, and she felt wonderfully at peace. This was how the world must have been long ago. Closing her eyes, she turned her face to the sun and allowed the gentle evening breeze to touch her face.

And then her eyes snapped open as icy fingers touched her flesh. Cold hard nails scraped gently against her forehead, brushing across her eyelids.

It was a branch, nothing more than a branch above her head, dipping in the breeze.

Smiling with relief, Karen closed her eyes again and tilted her face to the sun, feeling the light orange and red against her closed eyelids. The warmth enfolded her in a blanket and sleep came almost immediately.

She was dreaming.

But this was one of those terrible dreams where she knew she was dreaming, and was unable to do anything about it. She was sitting on the ground beneath the oak tree, but it was a lot smaller now, little more than a sapling, bending and twisting in an icy breeze coming in off the sea. She tried to stand, but she was unable to move. She was unable to turn her head, but at the very edges of her vision she could see the castle and church directly below. There was something wrong with the buildings . . .

She was dreaming.

Something was wrong. The castle and church were both in perfect repair, looking strong and solid, the cut stones bright, the edges sharp and clean, the slate roofs gleaming. Karen could hear voices. Adult voices, but she was unable to distinguish whether male or female. They were speaking in a strange, guttural, almost sing-song language which might have been Irish.

And then a child ran past, close enough to startle her and set her heart racing, bringing a lump to her throat. With her eyes, Karen followed the girl as she ran along a narrow track towards the church. The girl was no more than ten or eleven, with long, yellow-white hair streaming out behind her as she ran. She was wearing a simple dress of some coarse material, belted around her slender waist with a rope. She was barefoot, her feet and legs encrusted with dried mud, and the quick glimpse Karen had of the child's face showed it also smeared with mud.

There was movement to the left. Karen swivelled her eyes as three girls appeared. Two were obviously related, with the same dark hair, the same black eyes, the same coarse features. The third girl was blond, like the child who was running. They were all dressed in woollen robes, and were very dirty, with leaves and twigs entangled in their hair. There was a long ugly scratch on the blond girl's arm; all had scratches on their bare arms and legs, in fact. They were carrying bundles of wood on their backs, huge bundles that dwarfed the young women who bore them.

They passed within a few feet of Karen, but didn't look at her, didn't even acknowledge her presence.

And when she tried to speak, the words froze in her throat and her mouth refused to work.

She was dreaming.

She hoped if she kept repeating that, she would wake up. The dream wasn't frightening, not really terrifying like some ghastly monster-ridden nightmare. But the terrible feeling of helplessness disturbed her. She was an observer only; she could do nothing.

Then yet another girl appeared, coming from the direction of the castle. Unlike the others, this girl seemed to be staring directly at Karen. Red hair; Karen saw a mass of red hair surrounding a pale face. She couldn't make out the girl's features, but she knew the eyes would be green . . . because the face was familiar.

She was dreaming.

She had seen the face before. Recently.

The red-haired girl approached; knelt before her. She was wearing a long, high-necked, long-sleeved gown woven of fine soft wool, the edges of the neck and sleeves worked in an ornate Celtic pattern. A string of irregular amber beads encircled her neck and there was a thick silver bracelet on either arm. A jewelled dagger dangled from the broad belt that hung low over her hips.

And her eyes were green.

The girl spoke, her words savage, barbaric, changing a dozen times as she tried different languages, until finally the meaning of the sentences seemed to slide and shift and click into place in Karen's head.

"Yes . . . I can see you . . . but you should ask yourself . . . are you dreaming of me . . . or am I dreaming of you?"

And then the red-haired girl leaned forward, her fingers reaching for Karen's throat. As she did so, she opened her mouth and smiled. Her teeth were terrifying.

CHAPTER TWENTY

Robert held the girl until the shaking stopped . . . although he wasn't really sure who was shaking more; Karen or himself.

With Byte at his heels, he had been wandering around the ruined chapel, wondering what he was going to do next, when he suddenly became aware that the dog was growling softly. When he dropped his hand on to the German Shepherd's head, he realised that the short hairs on the back of her neck were stiff. The dog probably smelled rabbits in the fields. "Don't be silly . . ." he began.

And then the scream lanced through the early evening air. Robert shouted himself, the sound an involuntary reaction. Byte's growling turned to a whimper. Birds exploded out of the tower, cawing raucously. Robert was running towards the source of the sound even before its last echoes had died away. He hadn't recognised the voice – he had never heard anyone scream like that in his entire life – but he knew it had to be Karen, and also knew that it was a scream of mortal terror.

He found her huddled at the base of an ancient oak tree that stood on a knoll of land above the ruined church. The girl was curled into a foetal position, knees drawn up to her chest, head ducked down, forearms covering her face. He fell to his knees beside her, but when he touched her she flinched away with a wordless whimper.

"Karen . . . it's me . . . Karen? . . . it's Robert. Can you hear me, Karen?" He reached for her again, unaware that there were tears on his face. When his hand brushed her cheek she gasped, but didn't pull away this time. Lowering her arm, she peered at him with one wild eye.

"Karen . . . what's wrong? . . . Are you hurt? . . . Have you hurt yourself? . . . Can you talk to me, tell me what's happened?" Slowly, carefully, he sat on the ground alongside the girl, and put his back against the oak tree. Then he stretched out his hand and ran it over the girl's hair, brushing strands back off her face. When she didn't attempt to pull away, he leaned over and gathered her into his arms and held her until the shaking subsided.

They both jumped when Byte came padding up. The girl eased herself out of Robert's comforting embrace and wrapped her arms around the dog's neck, burying her face in its fur.

"I'm sorry," she said eventually, her voice muffled and soft. Not looking at Robert, her face still pressed to the dog's side, she said, "I fell asleep, and had a dream . . . a nightmare."

"How did you get up here?" he asked.

Karen took several long moments before she answered, "I don't know."

"Do you remember cycling down to the church with Byte?"

She started to nod, but then shook her head. "No."

"What is the last thing you remember?"

"I woke up in my bed at home from some terrible dream. I think I remember talking to my mother."

"Do you remember telling her that you and I had agreed to meet here?"

"I didn't tell her that . . . did I?"

"You did. And then you cycled down here, dumped your bike against the wall and went off, leaving poor Byte by herself. I guess she stayed to guard your bike."

Karen took a deep, shuddering breath. "Robert, I don't know what's happening to me. I don't remember any of that. I keep having these terrible dreams, these awful flashes . . ." She turned to point to the chapel. "I had the most bizarre dream. I was sitting here, right where you are in fact, but it was in another time. The church and castle were new, and the people were wearing old-fashioned clothes like in another age.

"Though I could see them, they couldn't see me. Except for this one girl." Karen frowned. "At least I think she was a girl . . . though now that I think back on it, she might have been older. There was something about her . . ." She drew a long, shuddering breath. "She *could* see me. She came right up to me, knelt here and looked into my face. I remember she had a mane of red hair and bright green eyes. She spoke to me . . . or at least I think she spoke . . . but maybe I was hearing her inside my head. And she asked me . . . she asked me if I was dreaming of her or if she was dreaming of me."

"Weird dream," Robert murmured.

Karen didn't hear him. "And then she leaned close and opened her mouth . . ." Her breath was coming quicker now and her heart was thumping in her chest. Unconsciously her fingers touched her throat, and she winced where they touched bruised flesh. "And then she bit me."

Robert drew up his knees and rested his chin on them. In the distance, Dublin was slowly coming alight, tiny spots of coloured light winking into existence. There was a question he had to ask Karen, but he was almost afraid to ask. Yet her symptoms reminded him of someone he knew . . . one of the kids from school . . .

"Karen," he said very quietly, "I have to ask you a question. And please, don't take this the wrong way. And I want you to know that however you answer, I'll believe you."

The girl raised her head to look at him. In the gathering twilight, his boyish features had become indistinct, his eyes deepened into shadow. She thought she caught a glimpse of what he might look like as a man.

"Are you taking drugs, Karen?"

The question hung in the air between them, poisoning the clean air.

Robert took a deep breath. He was aware that his relationship with Karen and their future together would depend on the girl's answer.

Karen's first reaction was to strike out. She had never been so insulted in her life. Just what sort of girl did he think she was? And then she steadied herself and calmed down. He had every reason for his suspicions. She had been acting strangely and her dreams were so bizarre, just like she imagined drug-induced hallucinations would be.

At least he cared enough to ask.

"No, Robert," she told him earnestly. "I know what this must sound like . . . I know what I sound like even to me, but I've never taken drugs. Nothing stronger than an aspirin anyway," she added with a wry smile.

Robert reached out and she put her hand in his.

"I believe you," he said simply.

"But what's wrong with me?" She was unable to keep the anguish, the fear from her voice and he wrapped his arms around her again, holding her tightly. "My aunt Rosie went mad," she whispered. "Isn't madness hereditary?"

"You're not going mad," Robert said with as much confidence as he could muster. "I think you're probably just coming down with some sort of fever. And it's been so hot lately you haven't been able to sleep, so you're overtired and that's why you're dreaming. You studied very hard just before the summer holidays for your exams. Maybe this is some sort of delayed stress."

Karen nodded. "You're right of course. That's all that's wrong. I'm tired, probably coming down with the flu. I'll have Mother take me to the doctor tomorrow and ask him for a tonic."

"Good idea." Her companion got slowly to his feet. "We should be getting back. We'll have to walk," he added, "I haven't any light on my bike, and I didn't expect to be out this late."

They collected their bikes and walked them back across the field towards the road. And somehow it seemed the most natural thing in the world for Robert to take Karen's hand.

And later, much later, when they reached Karen's gate,

it seemed even more natural for the girl to reach over and kiss him gently on the cheek. Both of them were glad it was dark.

Karen stood on the doorstep watching him until he rounded the corner, but instead of turning her key in the lock, she pushed her bike around the side of the house and disappeared into the shadows.

CHAPTER
TWENTY-ONE

B ob Carroll rolled over in bed, simultaneously reaching for the phone and looking at the digital alarm clock.

2:30 AM blinked in dim red letters.

"Yes," he mumbled, grabbing the receiver off the cradle of the phone on the locker, almost losing his grip on it as he struggled to sit up in bed.

Joyce Carroll rolled over and sat up. "Who is it at this hour?" she asked irritably.

"Who is this?" her husband echoed. Almost immediately he changed his tone, however. "Dermot . . . sorry, I didn't recognise your voice." Covering the mouthpiece, he glanced at his wife. "Dermot O'Sullivan."

Joyce frowned. Why was Dermot O'Sullivan, a man they barely knew, phoning at half past two in the morning?

"Karen?" She heard her husband say, and at once understood. Dermot O'Sullivan was Karen's father. "We haven't seen her all evening."

Joyce knew by the expression on Bob's face that something was wrong. Throwing back the duvet, she swung her legs out of bed and reached for her dressing gown.

"No, Robert is here," her husband was saying into the phone. "He came in as usual . . . well, a little later than usual," he added. "I'll ask him and phone you back."

When he hung up the receiver, his face was pale. "Karen's missing," he said without preamble. "She didn't come home at all this evening. They thought she was with Robert. When it got so late, they decided they'd better start phoning around."

Joyce Carroll pulled her dressing gown closed and tied the belt tightly around her waist. "I'll put the kettle on," she said. "Looks like it could be a long night."

Robert awoke with a start from a dream in which he had been digging something up, but with every spade of earth that he lifted from the hole, the edges crumbled further and more dirt cascaded in. The hole was filling faster than he could empty it.

Bright light from the lamp on his bedside locker hurt his eyes, and he sat up, shading them with his hand. He was surprised to find both his mother and father standing beside his bed. By the grim expressions on their faces he knew that something was wrong. They hadn't looked so serious since they learned of Aunt Maggie's death.

"What's wrong?" he wanted to know, knuckling his eyes.

Bob Carroll remained standing, but his wife sat down on the edge of her son's bed. She took Robert's hand in hers, the simple gesture frightening him more than anything else.

"What's wrong?" he asked again.

His father replied, "I've just had a call from Dermot O'Sullivan."

Dermot O'Sullivan? Robert had to think for a moment; he didn't know Dermot O'Sullivan. Was it someone he went to school with? Then he remembered – Karen's father.

"Karen didn't come home tonight," his mother said gently. "The O'Sullivans thought – hoped, I suppose – that she was with you."

Something cold and icy settled in the pit of Robert's stomach, something that deposited a bitter taste at the back of his throat. "I left her home," he said, wide-eyed. "I saw her to the door before I came back here." His voice was a hoarse whisper, lips and mouth abruptly dry. His tongue felt huge in his mouth.

"What time was that, Robert?" his father wanted to know.

"Ten-thirty . . . something like that."

Bob Carroll nodded. He knew the boy had come in by 10:45.

"But what do you mean, Karen didn't come home?" the boy asked tensely. " I left her there myself. I saw her go in . . ." he began, then realised he hadn't actually seen her enter her house. His last memory of her was of her standing on the doorstep, waving to him.

"And how was she at that time?" his mother asked.

"She was . . ." What was he going to say? Could he tell them that she had had an hallucination, a dream, that she was acting strange and weird, that he had even suspected she might be using drugs? "She was fine," Robert said, not meeting his parents' eyes.

"You didn't have a fight or anything?" Joyce Carroll persisted.

"No. Nothing like that."

"I'd better phone Dermot now," decided Robert's father. "He was waiting to hear from us before he phoned the police. I wish we had something more positive to tell him, though."

"The police!" Robert whispered.

Just then the phone rang, startling them.

Bob Carroll dashed into the master bedroom, followed moments later by his wife and son. They stood in the doorway, listening.

"Dermot! Robert says that Karen . . . Oh? You mean she's back?"

The sense of relief that washed over Robert actually left him feeling weak and trembling.

"Where was she . . . until this hour? I see. Well, our Robert says he left her to your door at ten-thirty. No, they didn't have a fight or anything. Yes, it is very strange," he agreed. "Look, it's no problem, we're all just delighted that she's safe and well. Goodnight." He hung up, turned to his wife and son and shrugged. "She turned up a few minutes ago. Said she'd simply gone for a walk on the beach."

Joyce put her arm around her son and steered him back towards his own room. In a low voice she asked, "You're sure you didn't have a fight?"

"No." His throat was so tight he could barely speak.

"Well, don't worry about it now. Go back to bed and try to get some sleep. I'll talk to Catherine O'Sullivan in the morning; maybe she'll have a better idea what this is all about by then."

"I . . . I don't suppose I could phone her, could I . . . see if she's all right?"

Joyce Carroll shook her head. "I don't think so. It's far too late and I'd imagine she has a lot of explaining to do."

CHAPTER
TWENTY-TWO

Was this a dream?

She wasn't sure . . . and she didn't really care. She was tired. So tired. All she wanted to do was to lie down and go to sleep. But if she slept she would dream and if she dreamed . . . it was all becoming so confusing. If *this* was a dream, could she then have a dream *within* a dream?

"You owe us an explanation, girl!" Dermot O'Sullivan brought his hand flat down on the kitchen table, the sound like a gunshot in the silence. "You had your mother worried half to death."

Karen raised her head to look at her father, struggling to focus on his furious face. If this was a dream, then none of this was important. But if it wasn't a dream, if this was real, then why was her father so angry? What had she done to upset him?

Turning slightly, she looked out of the kitchen window. Just beyond the pane, peering in at her, the red-haired girl waited.

"This is getting us nowhere," Catherine O'Sullivan said wearily. "Let's all go to bed now; we can talk about this again in the morning. Maybe Karen will be able to give us some answers then."

Dermot O'Sullivan started to shake his head, but Catherine ushered her daughter through the door and down the hall. "Are you all right?" she asked when they were out of the room. "Did . . . did anything happen to you?"

"I'm fine, really. I just . . . I just wanted some time to . . . to think and walk . . . and think."

"Is everything all right between you and Robert?"

"Everything is fine. Couldn't be better."

"Would you like to have a shower before you go to bed?" Catherine asked, pushing open the bedroom door.

With no surprise, Karen noticed that the red-haired girl was now hovering outside her bedroom window. The figure shook its head from side to side as if in response to Mrs O'Sullivan's question.

"No Mum," said Karen. "I'm so tired, I don't want a shower. I think I just want to sleep."

"I'll help you get undressed," Catherine began, but Karen pushed her away. "No! No, I can do it myself. I'm not a child anymore," she added emphatically, throwing herself on to the bed. "I wish everybody would remember that."

"As you wish," her mother said in a hurt voice. She bent to drop a swift kiss on top of Karen's head before the girl could pull away. There was a distinct smell of sea-salt in her hair, so perhaps the story about walking on the beach was true.

What Catherine O'Sullivan wanted to know, however, was whether she had been alone or not. If someone was with her – and that someone not Robert – then who? And for what purpose?

Karen waited until her mother had left the room and the door closed behind her. The girl got to her feet then, though she was bone tired, crossed to the window and pushed it open. Chill night air flooded into the room. Turning around, she went over to the dressing table and sat down before it. Picking up the bone comb Robert had given her, she began to ease the tangles from her hair. The long-toothed comb hissed through the blond strands.

When the face looked over her shoulder Karen didn't even jump. Without a word the red-haired girl took the bone comb from her suddenly cold fingers and began to comb her hair. Karen could hear a static crackle and feel a gentle tug on the tangles. "Am I dreaming?" she whispered hoarsely.

"Does it matter?"

"Yes, it matters. I have to know if this is a dream."

Watching Karen in the mirror, the red-haired girl smiled, but only with a slight curling of her lips. She didn't open her mouth and her green eyes were as cold as the sea. *"Some of this is a dream."*

"Am I dreaming of you?"

"Or I of you?" suggested the intruder, continuing to comb Karen's hair with slow, rhythmic strokes. *"We are dreaming of one another, actually. We are linked, you and I, by one of the oldest ties known to mankind, the bond of blood. We are almost sisters."*

"What do you mean?"

"You are almost of my family. Soon you will join me, free me."

"Join you? Where?" Karen became vaguely aware of someone knocking on her door, and her mother's voice calling her name. But it didn't seem important. She was curiously numb.

The red-haired girl stopped combing for a moment and turned to scowl at the door. Then Karen distinctly heard the lock click shut.

"There is something you must do for me," the stranger murmured, her hands moving hypnotically on Karen's hair once more. *"For us,"* she added.

"What?" The pounding on the door increased, and now her father's voice was clearly audible. "Do you hear me, young woman? Unlock this door at once!"

Slowly, as if in a dream, Karen turned to look towards the noise. When she turned back, the red-haired girl had disappeared. The bone comb caught in Karen's long hair was the only evidence that she had ever been in the room.

Later, much later, in the still grey hours just before the dawn, Karen dreamed that she was lying in a long stone box, dreaming of a girl lying on a narrow bed.

Who was dreaming of whom?

And when she finally opened her eyes, she was convinced that she was going to see the underside of the pitted stone slab inches from her nose. It was almost a shock to find the pale blue bedroom ceiling many feet above her head.

CHAPTER
TWENTY-THREE

In his youth James Bacon had exercised on this beach every dawn. In those days he had been able to run from one end to the other in twelve minutes, and at the peak of his fitness, shortly after he had come out of the army, he even managed it in nine minutes. Nowadays, if he was very lucky, he could do it in an hour, or an hour and a half if he had to sit down and rest before the end. This was happening more and more frequently, while his breath laboured in his lungs and his heart sent warning tingles into his left arm, numbing his fingertips.

James had lived in Skerries for most of his seventy-two years, with the exception of the time he had spent in the British Army. When he was growing up Skerries had been little more than a seaside fishing village. Then it grew into a small town popular during the summer months with holidaymakers, many of whom came from Northern Ireland.

In the 1950s and '60s Skerries had blossomed with the creation of the Red Island Holiday Camp, which could take five hundred guests. James had worked in the camp during the season, and worked on the fishing boats as well

– always saving his money. He could not remember a time he did not have a roll of notes in a jam jar under his bed.

When the camp eventually closed – cheap overseas flights had destroyed the concept of the holiday camp – many people had predicted that Skerries would return to being nothing more than a sleepy village. But not James.

He had watched the growth of Dublin, observed the way similar cities elsewhere had grown to absorb the surrounding towns and villages, and knew that sooner or later Skerries would become little more than a suburb of the capital. With what he had saved from his army pay and the contents of more than one jam jar, he began quietly buying up land close to the town. By listening to all the local gossip he learned who had financial trouble, who was likely to sell cheap, who wanted to go somewhere else. He told no one, aside from his solicitor and his estate agent, what he was doing. He continued to live a simple life and spent hardly anything on himself.

And he waited.

In the building boom of the late Seventies and early Eighties, James Bacon had become a wealthy man. He shrewdly invested what he had made out of property and became still more wealthy. Everything he touched seemed to turn to gold.

But his rapidly multiplying wealth hadn't brought him any real happiness. Instead, the money had made him arrogant, and his arrogance had lost him his few real friends. Sure, he had lots of people who called themselves his friends, especially in the pubs, where he bought round after round of drink though he didn't drink himself. But he knew these people for what they were and knew that when he died, no one would mourn him. Except perhaps his dogs.

James Bacon had always loved dogs.

He could clearly remember his first dog, a black and white mongrel pup whom he'd called Tiger, although Tiger was really a cat's name. Tiger had been followed by Buster, then Laurel and Hardy, twin Dobermans. In the army he'd volunteered to take care of his unit's mascot, an enormous Irish wolfhound named Cu, which was the Irish for dog.

In England they'd always pronounced it as *Coo*. The dog didn't mind. But James did. He was very proud of Cu, who loved him in return and slept at the foot of his cot. Cu didn't care whether or not James had any money.

The old man nudged a shell on the beach with his walking stick and smiled. All his *friends* were going to be terribly surprised and disappointed when they discovered that he was leaving his fortune to the Cats and Dogs Home.

James paused, leaning on his stick, and turned to look out across the sea, willing his racing heart to slow down. He had suffered his first attack ten years ago; two years later he'd had his second. The doctors had given him a triple by-pass then and advised him to change his lifestyle, relax his hectic pace. But by that time he had business interests throughout western Europe. Changing his lifestyle was impossible; most of his business meetings seemed to take place over dinner. The food was always rich and he simply couldn't find the time to exercise.

His third heart attack had nearly killed him.

The day he got out of hospital, he'd sold everything

and retired to the village of his birth. Except that Skerries was no longer a village; it was a thriving town almost on the outskirts of rapidly expanding Dublin. It amused him to see all the houses that had been built on the land he once owned. Thousands of them. Each one representing money in his pocket.

Now he lived a quiet life, reading, watching television, wandering around the beach and town, looking after his dogs. He had three dogs these days, small dogs who didn't need much exercise. They were named after the three Marx Brothers – Groucho, Chico and Harpo. He ran the back of his hand across his forehead. What was the name of the fourth Marx brother . . . Zeppo? That was it. Zeppo. Maybe he'd get another dog and call it Zeppo.

There was something bobbing in the sea just off shore . . .

James shaded his eyes and squinted, trying to make out the shape against the sparkling water, but the sun coming over the horizon was shining directly into his eyes. He shrugged, losing interest. The thing was probably no more than a piece of seaweed or a lobster pot broken free of its moorings.

The old man continued down the beach, but occasionally he glanced back at the object floating in the water. To his surprise, it seemed to keep pace with him. He stopped again, his curiosity aroused. Planting his walking stick firmly in the soft sand, he leaned both hands on it and concentrated on the object bobbing in the water.

A wave rolled in, bringing it closer. The thing rolled over and four limp legs bobbed on the water. The old man recognised it then. "Aaah no," he whispered.

James Bacon started forward, wading into the

shallows, ignoring the water that lapped over his £200 Italian loafers. Crouching, he grabbed one of the legs and hauled the creature out of the water.

It was a dog.

He could not tell what breed it was. It lay on the beach like an empty sack, looking tiny and shrivelled, eyes wide and glassy.

The old man felt tears start to his own eyes. The death of an animal always moved him. He had once broken a man's arm because he had found him beating a dog.

Kneeling in the sand, James ran practised hands over the dog's sodden fur, feeling for broken bones, looking for an injury. He could find nothing. Maybe the dog had slipped off the pier and drowned and . . . his fingers touched a series of tiny punctures in the dog's throat.

Pulling away the clotted fur, he discovered nine perfectly circular holes that ran the length of the jugular vein.

It was close to eight o'clock by the time the old man returned home. Unable to carry the dog back with him, and unwilling to leave it on the beach, he had finally compromised and gently placed the small limp body among the sand dunes, close to a set of wooden steps. He was going home to change his ruined shoes and soaking socks, then get into his car and return for the dog. He simply couldn't leave it to be dumped into a trash can or torn apart by the gulls.

"I'm home," he called, turning the key in the lock and stepping into the tiled hallway. Usually there would be a patter of feet as the dogs scrambled to meet him . . . but not this morning. "You lazy things," he said good-naturedly, stepping into the kitchen. The dog-flap in the kitchen door that led out on to the paved patio was half open; the dogs were probably snoozing in the early morning sunshine. Standing at the sink, he sipped a glass of water while he swallowed two tiny white pills. He took so many tablets now that he almost forgot what some of them were for.

There was a cardboard box in the garage, he'd use that to carry the dead dog back home. Then he'd bury it in the orchard, where all of his pet dogs were buried. Sometimes, when he felt particularly lonely, he'd go into the orchard and talk to them.

Living or dead, they were his friends.

James Bacon pulled open the kitchen door and looked out. "I'm home boys," he began . . . and then stopped.

The three dogs were lying scattered across the patio, and he knew from their terrible stillness and unnatural postures that they were dead.

Trembling violently, the old man sank to his knees beside the oldest dog, Groucho, and touched its fur. It was still warm; the dog hadn't been dead long. He lifted the dog in his arms and cradled it to his chest. It felt so small and light; weighing hardly anything.

When he gently traced its bones, and prodded its stomach, he could discover no injury at all, nothing broken, none of the muscular rigidity poison causes, no blood around its muzzle. And then he discovered the nine puncture marks on its throat.

All the dogs carried the same marks. Nine tiny holes. But there was no blood.

Anywhere.

CHAPTER
TWENTY-FOUR

"And finally on this lunchtime news, a bizarre series of dog deaths has occurred in the seaside town of Skerries, twenty miles north of Dublin. The bodies of fifteen dogs have been discovered, while another eight household pets are missing, presumed dead. There are no external injuries on the dead animals and early tests have ruled out poisoning. Local residents are concerned that the dogs may have died from toxic gases or radioactive material escaping from the British nuclear fuel plant at Sellafield, which lies almost directly opposite Skerries across the Irish Sea.

"Police have denied as ludicrous, rumours that all of the dogs were drained of blood. The investigation is ongoing.

"This is Niall Mulligan, RTE Lunchtime News."

CHAPTER
TWENTY - FIVE

She was stronger now.

Not as strong as she would be, nor as strong as she could be. The dogs' blood – thin and sour, without the complex energy of the humankind – would not sustain her long, but it lent her enough strength to allow the withered skin on her ancient bones to begin to regenerate.

Wrinkled flesh had filled out, grown smooth and fresh. Thin lips had expanded to cover overlong yellow teeth. A mass of flaming red hair had sprouted from her scalp, writhing with a life of its own as it grew and thickened. Wispy strands of grey hair fell away as the new growth came in.

Eyes opened.

Milky white, with no coloured iris, they stared unseeing at the lid of the coffin inches away. Once, long ago, when the cruel human kind had put her in this stone tomb, she had been forced to stare at the stone slab every minute of every day for more than sixty human years until at last The Sleep had overtaken her. The Sith did not need light to see by and she had come to know every inch of that slab, every tiny imperfection, the patterns of the silica, the speckles of crystal embedded in the rock. Know and hate them all.

A tendril of colour snaked across her white eyes.

When the Sith slept their metabolism decreased dramatically, so that to an uninformed observer it might look as if they were dead. Their huge, tri-chambered hearts slowed almost to a stop, their hair and nails ceased growing, and their sensitive eyes developed a milky, cataract-like protective shell.

To reawaken their sleeping bodies they needed blood. A single drop was sufficient to begin the process, but to complete the awakening they would need much more.

Now a spiderweb of thinnest crimson threads spread across the vampyre's blind white eyes. Her awakening had begun three days ago when a single drop of human blood – thin and weakened by its journey through the soil – had finally reached her. That one drop, no more than a tiny speckle, had been enough. Its power, the power of life, had dragged her back from the Dreamscape and returned her consciousness to this stone box deep underground.

Tasting the blood, feeling it burn and shiver on her tongue and knowing that there was no more, had been maddening. For a while she had thrashed and howled in the darkness.

Slowly her eyes filled with blood, dissolving the protective white shell. Rivulets of dark red curled in crimson tears down the side of her face, running along the rims of her ears before disappearing into her hair.

Wherever it touched her flesh, the blood hissed.

When a semblance of sanity returned, she began to plan her escape.

Using skills she had developed and honed in the Dreamscape, she had prepared to send her spirit out into the world above, wandering through the dreams of the humans, watching and learning.

Strega blinked away the last of the blood. Now her eyes were alive, with irises of a bright grass-green, centred with slitted pupils like those of a cat. The teeth behind her thin lips were long and white and needle-sharp, and her tongue was red and pointed.

And she was hungry.

Terribly hungry.

She found the boy first. A comb that had once belonged to her led her to him. Only then was she aware that one of her pair of matched combs was missing. It must have fallen out when she was being bundled into the coffin all those years ago. In any other time, in any other circumstance, forfeiting the comb would have been a devastating loss. But not here and not now. The comb provided a tangible link between her physical body which lay in the coffin, and her dream presence which haunted the boy.

The comb allowed her to lock on to him, to watch over him from the Dreamworld, waiting like a huge spider until he should fall asleep, and she could invade his dreams. But before she had a chance to strike, he had given the comb to the girl.

In the Dreamscape, the vampyre's laugh echoed and re-echoed across the grey emptiness. One victim would do as well as another.

Encouraging the tired girl to use the comb was simplicity itself. And once the comb had tasted the girl's blood, she was Strega's creature.

In the coffin the transformation was almost complete. The withered, mummy-like remains of an ancient being had been replaced by the image of a beautiful young woman with white flesh, green eyes and a mass of bright red hair. Only slitted pupils and concealed fangs indicated that this was no human.

Rolling over in the confined space, the vampyre closed her hand into a fist and pounded it against the floor of the coffin. Ancient stone chipped. She struck again, hammering until the stone turned to gritty powder.

When the coffin had been built by the masons all those years ago, the priests had sealed the edges with their blessed names and inscribed a Christian Cross on the lid – as if that would have any effect on a creature who had been ancient before the White Christ walked the earth. But in spite of all their precautions, they had overlooked protecting the base of the coffin.

CHAPTER
TWENTY-SIX

"What's wrong?" Karen asked sharply.

Robert turned to look at her, unable to keep the surprise from his face.

Karen nudged a stone with her foot, then stooped down to pick up a tiny shell. Blowing sand from the shell, she slipped it into her pocket. "You've barely spoken a word to me since we left home," she said. Her voice was cold with hurt. Walking away from him, she sat down on a flat rock, leaned back on her elbows and stared down the deserted beach. Beyond her profile, the Mountains of Mourne were clearly visible against the distant sky.

Robert didn't know what to say. It was hard to know how a girl might take things, he thought. There were a dozen questions he wanted to ask – he simply couldn't find the right one.

He hadn't had much sleep last night. He'd tossed and turned, wondering what was wrong with Karen, wondering where she'd been. On the couple of occasions when he did slip into a light doze, he found himself hearing once more what Peter Kater had told him about seeing Karen with Paddy Ellis.

Robert had been going to ask her about it, but with the strangeness at the ruined chapel, the opportunity had never presented itself.

"Well?" she snapped. "You didn't bring me all the way out here *not* to talk to me, did you?"

When he'd called for her just after noon, he had suggested that they cycle up to Barnageera, where they could talk in private. But there was something about Karen this morning . . . something different . . . something he couldn't quite put his finger on. She'd changed her hair; maybe that was it. She wasn't wearing it swept back from her face in its usual tight ponytail. Now it hung loose and billowed around her shoulders, looking too glamorous for her years.

She was wearing make-up too – something she very rarely did. It heightened her cheekbones and subtly changed the contours of her face. Against her pale skin, her eyes were sunken and darkly shadowed.

"Did you get in a lot of trouble about last night?" he asked, eventually.

"Not much. My folks weren't terribly pleased, but there was little they could do, was there? It's my life after all."

Her defiant attitude surprised him. "Where did you go?"

"For a walk. On the beach."

"Until two in the morning? Why didn't you tell me?" he asked, facing her squarely. "I would have come with you so you wouldn't be alone."

"I wanted to be alone." She smiled, the edges of her lips turning upwards, but it was a cold, almost unpleasant smile. "You can't come everywhere with me, you know. We're not joined at the hip like Siamese twins."

Robert turned away before he said something he would regret. She wasn't well, he kept telling himself; she wasn't well. That explained her irritable attitude. She hadn't slept a lot last night – he could tell that by her appearance – and she'd probably caught hell from her parents this morning. No wonder she was in a bad humour.

"I'm surprised your folks let you out today," he said, looking out to sea, where seagulls were diving on to a patch of seaweed.

"They don't know I'm out."

The boy whirled around to find her standing right behind him. "What?"

"In fact," the girl continued, smiling, "they told me that I wasn't to leave the house all day."

"But Karen . . . well, what *are* you doing here?"

"I'm old enough to make my own decisions," she said with a toss of her head. The heavy mane of hair swung with the gesture.

Reaching out, he caught both her arms above the elbows, but she abruptly shook herself free. For a moment the look on her face – anger, disgust, and something else, something completely alien – shocked him.

"Don't you ever touch me!" she spat.

"Karen I . . . " he began.

The girl spun on her heel and walked away.

"Karen . . . what's happening to you?"

"I'm growing up," she said over her shoulder without looking back.

Robert trailed after her slowly. He felt completely at a

loss. The change in her was so surprising, so abrupt. Perhaps she really was taking drugs after all. One of the first signs of drug abuse was an abrupt personality change, irrational anger, sudden mood swings. Karen was demonstrating all of these.

Falling into step beside her, wondering if he should voice his suspicions to his parents, Robert said, "Did you hear what happened in town last night? Loads of dogs died mysteriously, and more are missing."

"I know," said Karen shortly.

"How?" The question just popped out, without thinking.

"I beg your pardon?"

He caught her arm again, and this time forced her to turn and look at him. "How did you hear about it?"

Karen's expression was unreadable.

"You were still in bed when I got to your place," Robert said, thinking hard. "Remember? You'd just woken up. While you were dressing I heard about the dogs for the first time on the one o'clock news. But you were having a shower then, so you couldn't have heard."

"It must have been an earlier news broadcast," she said quickly, wrenching her arm free, turning and striding off down the beach.

Robert watched her go. He'd heard both the eleven and the twelve o'clock news . . . and neither had made any mention of the dogs.

He raced after Karen, determined to confront her with this, determined to try and get at the truth – whatever the truth was.

When he caught up with her she was standing on a

seaweed-draped boulder and gazing out to sea, concentrating on some floating rubbish under attack from the gulls. She was staring so intently that Robert followed her gaze . . . and realised that what he had taken for rubbish was in fact the corpse of a dog in the water. A German Shepherd.

"Karen?" he whispered, looking at the girl. "Where was Byte this morning?"

There was something wrong with her face. It looked as if the muscles beneath the skin were shifting, moving, one half of her mouth trying to smile, the other twitching nervously. Her left eye was bright and hard, while tears leaked from her right eye.

The trembling began then, a shuddering that started low in her hips and moved up her body in long waves, until she wrapped her arms around her ribs and hugged herself tightly in an effort to stop it. But she could not. When the shuddering rose above her chest and rippled through her throat muscles, she opened her mouth and screamed.

The gulls shrieked in mocking echo as the withered body of Byte was washed ashore in a tangle of seaweed.

Karen screamed and screamed, flailing wildly at Robert when he attempted to get close to her.

After a while her screams began to sound uncomfortably like laughter.

CHAPTER
TWENTY-SEVEN

"I've given her a mild sedative," explained Doctor Elliott as he pulled the bedroom door closed behind him. The silver-haired doctor followed Catherine O'Sullivan into the sitting-room, where young Robert Carroll was sitting facing Karen's father. Without being asked, the doctor sank into an overstuffed grey leather armchair.

"You'll have some tea, Steven?" Catherine asked.

"Tea would be fine." He watched as she left the room, then the big man leaned back into the chair, stretched his legs out and crossed them at the ankle. He knew the O'Sullivans well; he and Dermot were both members of the Skerries Golf Club, and he sat on the school Board of Governors with Catherine.

Glancing at Robert, he asked Dermot. "Can we talk freely in front of this young man?"

The boy felt colour rise to his cheeks; it was a long time since someone had spoken about him as if he were not even in the room.

Dermot O'Sullivan reached out and squeezed Robert's arm. "You can speak in front of Robert. He phoned me, and he looked after Karen until I arrived. He's a responsible youngster and he and Karen are good friends."

The doctor leaned forward. He brushed strands of hair back off his high forehead with a practised movement, revealing a thick gold watch on his left wrist. There was an equally heavy gold bracelet on his right wrist. When he smiled he revealed a mouthful of gleaming white teeth that looked far too perfect to be anything but the most expensive dentures.

Robert decided at that moment that he didn't like the doctor. He knew Karen had no time for Jean, Dr Elliott's daughter, who was in her class in school.

"Just how is Karen?" Dermot wanted to know.

"Physically, she's fine," replied the doctor. "She's in perfect health. Temperature normal, blood-pressure excellent, heart-rate regular. I have, ah, taken some blood samples, however, and I've asked Catherine to get me a urine sample as soon as Karen wakes up. I'll have them analysed. They may tell us . . . what the problem is."

"You make it sound as if you're looking for something in particular," Dermot O'Sullivan remarked.

Steven Elliott leaned back in the chair and brushed an imaginary hair from the thigh of his expensive trousers. "I've been a doctor a long time. I've learned that the most obvious diagnosis is often the answer.

"What we have here is a perfectly normal, healthy girl who suddenly begins behaving irrationally, very much out of character." Holding up a tanned hand, Elliott began to tick off points on his fingers. "Catherine told me Karen stayed out until nearly three o'clock in the morning, and refused to give an adequate explanation.

Today you ordered her to remain in the house, yet she deliberately disobeyed you to go off with this . . . *boy*. Again, out of character. The next thing we know she's hysterical, shaking as if she's having a fit and virtually incoherent. Has anything like that ever happened with her before?"

Dermot O'Sullivan shook his head. "Never."

"Has she ever wilfully disobeyed you?"

"No."

"Has she ever had one of these screaming, shivering attacks before?"

"Never."

"Well, I'll tell you what I think," said the doctor, knotting his hands together and indicating Robert with his eyes. "I don't know this young man, he's not one of my patients. But I suspect you'll find he's at the back of all this. Young people today, they begin to experiment with all sorts of substances. Sometimes they need encouragement, and a friend gives it to them. A friend like this boy, for example . . ."

"How dare you!" Robert surged to his feet. "Are you suggesting that Karen is taking drugs . . . and that I gave them to her!"

"It's a possibility," the doctor replied coldly. "A distinct possibility. We'll know more when the blood tests come back."

Robert had never been so angry in his life. His stomach was churning and a sudden headache throbbed behind his eyes. His cheeks blazed with fury as he told Elliott, "Karen does not take drugs. Neither do I. Even talking about it is . . . is disgusting. And to suggest that I would give them to her is . . . *wrong*. A lie. You can't go around saying things like that about people."

The doctor smiled blandly, unperturbed. "I would have expected you to react this way. Protest your innocence all you like, young man. But attacking me won't alter the facts. Karen was a fine healthy young woman until she met you. Now she's undergoing a distinct personality change. It doesn't take a genius to work out that you're the catalyst."

Robert was spluttering with indignation, but the doctor pressed on. "Go on, why don't you tell me that you love her, isn't that what you were going to say?"

The boy swallowed hard; he had been about to say those very words.

"Young people like you," Elliott snorted with contempt, "don't know what love is."

Robert took a deep breath, trying to calm himself. Ignoring the doctor, he turned to Dermot O'Sullivan, who had remained silent throughout the exchange. "Mr O'Sullivan, you have to believe me, Karen is not involved in drugs," he said earnestly. "Neither am I. I care too much for Karen – and I'd like to think that I'm too clever – to get involved in anything like that. You do believe me, don't you?"

Dermot O'Sullivan looked from the doctor's mildly amused sneer to Robert's deadly serious expression. He didn't want to believe that his daughter was involved in drugs, but he'd read so much recently about teenagers getting hooked. Cannabis, Ecstasy . . . even sniffing glue. And Karen had been acting very strange recently. He'd been shocked when Steven Elliott suggested drugs, equally shocked when he had implicated Robert. Yet it *did* make some sort of sense . . .

Slowly, Dermot O'Sullivan stood up to face Robert. For a long moment the man and the boy gazed at each other across the room. Robert held his chin up and his eyes steady, hoping Karen's father would read the truth in his face.

At last O'Sullivan stuck out his hand. "I believe you," he said simply. Glancing sidelong at the doctor he added, "I've always believed in innocent until proven guilty."

"I'll have those blood tests back tomorrow," the doctor snapped, angered because O'Sullivan was siding with the boy. He stood up as Catherine returned with the tea tray. "I've just remembered another appointment," he announced brusquely. "I'll phone you tomorrow . . . and fax you a copy of the blood test." He made it sound like a threat.

CHAPTER
TWENTY-EIGHT

Karen could hear their voices in the other room – though that should have been impossible. The walls of the O'Sullivan bungalow were thick, almost soundproof, and when she was in her bedroom she usually heard nothing that was going on in the rest of the house. Yet she still heard the voices.

Was she dreaming?

Was she imagining that she was listening to her father and the doctor she disliked so intensely chatting together? Did she really hear Robert's voice, high and angry . . . or was she imagining that too ?

She snuggled deeper under the bedclothes. Her thoughts were confused, made woolly by the injection the doctor had given her, but in spite of this Karen struggled to make sense of the past few hours.

There were so many gaps in her memory . . . so many places where she was unsure if she was remembering a real event or a dream.

Walking on the beach last night . . . no, she'd been splashing through the shallows, running wild and free with the sea wind blowing strands of bright red hair around her face.

But her hair wasn't red.

The night had been vibrant with sights and sounds and smells. The colours had been intense, and she saw hues she never saw normally. She heard sounds that were totally unfamiliar, part of a world she had never experienced. The fragrances of sea and sand and soil, green leaves and night blooming flowers filled her nostrils, each one individual and distinct.

But she had suffered from sinus since she was a child and her sense of smell had never been keen.

There was another odour too, a pungent, coppery smell like that of a butcher's shop. But she forced herself to ignore it. Not yet, said something inside her. Not yet. But soon.

Soon.

Gradually she became aware that dogs howled when she drew near them, the eerie sounds rising higher and higher until they soared past human hearing . . . but she could still hear them. She could understand them, comprehend their primal terror.

She relished their fear, almost tasting it, when she approached, moving stealthily, silently towards them, the bone comb in her hands.

Her kind had always feared the canines the human had adopted so readily.

Her kind?

Dogs could sense the Sith and reacted strongly to them. In the past the human kind had used hounds to track the Sith to their hidden lairs. Sith?

But the only pets the Sith had ever kept were felines. Cats were clever and independent; their love was hard to win, not given slavishly, foolishly, to just anyone. She herself had had scores of cats over the years . . .

She had always hated cats.

. . . though in truth they were more than pets, they were companions, fellow hunters, both preferring the hours of darkness, both returning with the first light of dawn, the blood of a kill still damp on their lips.

Karen rolled over in the bed, her breathing steady and regular, eyes moving behind the closed lids as she slipped deeper and deeper into sleep.

And while she slept she dreamed.

She dreamed she was in a long narrow box, trapped, but not afraid. She had rolled over in the box and was facing downwards. The box was stone, but the stone was cracked and chipped. Karen raised her hand and smashed it into the stone, sending chips flying. She knew she should feel pain from the blow, but there was no pain because this was a dream.

And she knew that the girl in the stone box was dreaming also . . . terrible, terrifying dreams.

Strega.

That was the sleeping girl's name.

In the quiet bedroom, Karen rolled over, dry lips forming a single word: *"Strega."*

CHAPTER
TWENTY-NINE

In truth, Steven Elliott was more amused than angry as he swung the black Mercedes out of the driveway, deliberately gunning the engine to scatter the carefully raked gravel.

Stupid, stupid people. He did not suffer fools gladly, and the O'Sullivans obviously were fools. Why wouldn't they simply accept the evidence before them? But this was how the evil of drugs spread . . . because people refused to accept the facts, even when they saw them with their own eyes.

Just as he had done with Simon.

The doctor's handsome face turned bitter as unconsciously he transferred his anger into the car, pushing the pedal to the floor, the speedometer edging upwards towards sixty.

Simon; eighteen years of age, a brilliant student with a career in medicine already mapped out for him, a safe, secure, wealthy future simply waiting for him to grasp it. He would be twenty-six this year – if he had lived. Twenty-six.

By the time Steven Elliott was twenty-six, he'd

completed his exams and was already working as a junior doctor in Great Ormond Street Children's Hospital. But Simon would never have been a junior doctor. Steven Elliott had wanted his son to specialise, maybe go into cosmetic surgery where the big money was, or biological research which could lead to lasting fame.

But then Simon had met the girl.

The doctor frowned. He couldn't even remember her name, the name of the girl who had killed his son. Oh, she hadn't shot or stabbed him, nothing so dramatic, though it might have been better if she had. No, her murderous crime was introducing Simon to drugs.

Of course Simon had always denied it, but Steven Elliott knew she was responsible. In a matter of days, Simon had gone from being a brilliant student to having absolutely no interest in his studies. He had always dressed neatly, but suddenly he had started wearing the most outrageous clothing. He'd even turned up with a tight haircut just like that boy – what was his name – Robert?

And he'd had lost all respect for his father.

The car lurched on a tight corner, spraying grit from its back wheels as the doctor turned on to the narrow coast road. Intent on his bitter memories, Steven Elliott was unaware that the needle on the speedometer was now brushing seventy.

For the best part of three months, he had ignored the evidence. Been wilfully blind, refused to believe. He'd put the change in Simon down to teenage rebelliousness, high spirits, to a hundred and one different things.

But when Simon had started staying out late at night –

just like Karen – his father had been unable to overlook his behaviour any longer. Simon had come home wild-eyed, filthy, reeking of some bitter smoke, and he'd known then. While the boy slept – aided by a sedative Steven Elliott had added to his drink – he'd gone through his son's room until he finally found what he was looking for: a handful of tiny white pills in a metal box behind a shelf of cheap horror novels.

Steven Elliott had known immediately where his son got the drugs – from the new girlfriend. She was the only thing in his life that was different: a dyed-red-haired girl with a sharp, inner-city accent.

After he found the pills, the doctor had tried to rouse his son to ask him about them. But when he shook the young man he found him cold and still.

The autopsy would show that Simon Elliott had died from an overdose of barbiturates. And Steven Elliott would never be able to shake off the fear that the sedative he'd added to his son's tea might have been the extra amount that killed him.

But no – he hadn't killed Simon, he couldn't let himself believe that. The red-haired girl, the one who'd introduced him to drugs in the first place, she was really responsible. If only he could get his hands on her . . .

There was a sudden flash of red to the left. A girl with flaming red hair. Darting into the middle of the road. Then just standing there. Waiting. Smiling.

The doctor stood on the brakes as he frantically spun the steering wheel to one side. The heavy car, now travelling at seventy-eight miles an hour, fishtailed, tyres failing to gain a purchase on the salt-slick coast road.

Steven Elliott fought to regain control but it was no use. The car slammed into the low sea-wall, crashing through it with a scream of tearing metal.

And then there was a long silence until the car struck the rocky beach far below and exploded into a ball of fire.

Karen O'Sullivan rolled over, thin lips curling into a smile that mirrored the smile on the creature in the stone coffin.

CHAPTER THIRTY

"Mum, I really don't want to go."

Joyce Carroll leaned across and pushed open the passenger door. The car immediately filled with that odour peculiar to fishing harbours everywhere: salt, diesel oil and fish.

"You're going," she told her son firmly. "You've been moping around the house all afternoon. It'll do you good to get out and besides, I've already paid for the tickets," she added.

Robert Carroll climbed reluctantly out of the car and slammed the door behind him. He walked around the front of the car and crouched down to look in through the driver's window. "I'll go on one condition," he said.

"And what's that?" Looking out at him, his mother squinted in the late afternoon sunshine. Fumbling in the glove box, she took out the sunglasses Robert had bought her for her last birthday. They were supposed to be genuine Ray Bans, but they'd only cost him five pounds, and it wasn't until much later when he'd seen the genuine article on sale for fifteen times that amount did he realise he'd been conned.

He glanced at them ruefully now as his mother put them on, his reflection distorted in the curved lenses.

"I'll go on condition that you don't come and collect me," he told her. "I'll make my own way home."

"It's a deal. On condition that you're home by midnight . . . or twelve-thirty at the very latest."

"Thanks, Mum."

His mother reached out and gave his hand a fond squeeze. "I know you were supposed to be going to this beach party with Karen, and I'm sorry she won't be here. But look – try and enjoy it. I'm sure Karen will be up and about in a day or two; you can have other parties together."

Robert nodded and stood back while his mother pulled away from the kerb, black exhaust leaking from the tail-pipe. With a sigh, he turned away and walked along the Harbour Road. The throbbing sounds of a rave beat were already pulsing on the warm air as the day drew on toward evening.

Originally the beach party had actually been held on the beach, but over the years, as people discovered the difficulty of dancing on soft sand, it had moved up on to the grass margin that bordered the beach. Then two years previously the venue had been changed to the car park that covered the area known as the Captains on Red Island.

The island was not actually an island at all any more. Enough land had been reclaimed from the sea to turn it into a small peninsula which had for many years been home to the Red Island Holiday Camp. When the camp had closed down, the place fell into disuse until it was re-designed and landscaped into a large carpark with spectacular seaward views north, east and south.

Robert had attended the party during the two previous years and hadn't enjoyed it much . . . but then, he hadn't gone with Karen. This year he'd really been looking forward to the occasion. But now . . .

Turning to the right, leaving the harbour behind him, he started up the road to the car park. A number of other young men and women, singly and in groups, were making their way up the road. Their conversation and laughter rang through the air as the shadows grew longer before them.

Robert met Peter Kater at the entrance to the car park. The boy's sallow face was flushed and, although there was supposed to be no alcohol at this party, the young man was holding a sweating can of cider in his hands. They nodded to one another.

"I suppose you heard?" Peter asked. He was speaking with the exaggerated preciseness of someone who knew they had drunk far too much.

"Heard what?"

"About Doctor Elliott, Jean Elliott's father."

"What about him?" Robert asked cautiously. Surely the doctor hadn't made his wild accusations public?

"Drove his car off the coast road this afternoon." Peter's free hand described an arc. "Straight into the beach. Gas tank exploded. Boom!" He laughed drunkenly and repeated "Boom!"

Robert took the can from Peter's hand and gulped the sour-tasting cider. Suddenly his mouth and throat were very dry. "When . . . when did this happen?"

Peter shrugged. "Sometime around two or three . . ."

The doctor had left the O'Sullivans' at around two-forty-five.

"Hey, are you all right? You look a bit green."

Robert handed back the can. "Must be the drink."

"I thought you were coming with your girlfriend?" Peter called as Robert walked away,

"She couldn't make it," Robert said over his shoulder, but not loud enough for Peter to hear. Peter's response was swallowed up as the music was cranked up.

Robert kept to the periphery of the crowd. The rotating lights around the DJ's desk illuminated the centre of the throng, leaving the edges in shadow. The orange glow of cigarettes and an occasional candle flame illuminated the now swiftly falling darkness.

Robert knew most of the people he saw, but tonight he didn't want to talk to any of them. He needed to think and, paradoxically, here in the midst of this huge crowd, with the music a solid pulse in the air, he found he could think. Shoving his hands deep into the back pockets of his jeans, he stared across the black waters of the Irish Sea towards the distant flash of the lighthouse and tried to make sense of the past few days.

Begin with what you know, he decided.

Karen had changed. Suddenly, dramatically and even physically. The girl he knew, the girl he loved – and even admitting it silently to himself made him blush – had become secretive and withdrawn, obsessed with weird dreams. He shuddered when he recalled the look on her face as she'd watched the pathetic body of Byte being washed ashore, and then those screams, those terrible, laughing screams . . .

Maybe Doctor Elliott was right, maybe she was taking drugs.

And now Doctor Elliott was dead. Where did that fit into the puzzle? Everyone was talking about it; he caught snatches of conversations around him. But no one seemed to think there was anything out of the ordinary about the crash. It seemed like nothing more than a tragic accident; the doctor had been driving too fast on the dangerous coast road and he'd lost control of the car. Some of those who had gone to see the wreck said that the skid marks stretched for more than a hundred yards.

And yesterday the dogs had been killed.

Everyone was talking about that too. Five of the missing dogs had turned up. Two had been washed ashore on the beach and one had been hauled up in the fishing nets. But only when people began discussing the dogs, comparing where they'd lived, did they realise that all the dogs lived in houses that backed on to the beach.

Someone had gone in, killed the dogs and then carried their bodies down to the beach to toss them into the water.

Why?

No one knew, but Robert heard one girl hiss in a frightened whisper that none of the dogs had any blood in them, they were completely drained.

Robert suddenly nodded in understanding. If the corpses were tossed into the sea, the lack of blood would not be so apparent.

Paddy Ellis!

He'd been found on the beach. Washed ashore. Just like the dogs. Robert began to shake his head. What he was thinking was inconceivable.

And Karen.

Somehow it all kept coming back to Karen.

Peter Kater had told him that he'd seen Karen with Paddy.

She'd been walking on the beach at dead of night when the dogs were killed. Her own dog had been one of them.

Yet she didn't seem to grieve.

The doctor had been attending her literally moments before he too died in mysterious circumstances.

Suddenly Robert felt cold, though the August evening was warm and windless. This was a chill that started deep in his stomach and percolated slowly outwards. He drew a deep, shuddering breath.

OK. So Karen was involved. He didn't know how or why, but he was absolutely certain that she was. And so was Baldungan Castle. He stared unseeingly out across the water as bits and pieces of the puzzle came together in his head, creating a terrible whole.

The first time Karen had acted strange was when she'd met him in Baldungan a couple of days ago. And then he'd found her there later, obviously distressed, unaware even how she'd got there.

The music in the background changed, slowed to a ballad that was currently advertising a brand of jeans. Karen looked good in jeans . . .

Right now Robert desperately needed someone he could talk to, someone he could trust, someone who wouldn't laugh at him if he was to tell them what he knew. He mentally ran through a list of his friends, but there was no one he trusted that much. And he couldn't tell his parents; he just couldn't. They might well think he was on drugs too, with such a story.

Maybe it was time to go back to Baldungan Castle for another look, a closer look.

When he turned around, he saw Karen.

For a moment he thought he was imagining her. Karen was at home in her bed, sleeping off the effects of a sedative Doctor Elliott had given her! But even before he started pushing his way through the swaying crowd, he knew that he was indeed looking at Karen.

The girl was dancing with a boy Robert knew only vaguely, a short, stocky, acne-covered boy who played rugby. They were dancing far too close together. When they turned, Robert could see the boy's broad, stubby-fingered hands pressing low against her back. They spun and he saw that her chin was resting on the boy's shoulder, her arms on either side of his head, stretched straight out, fingers folded tightly together.

The boy whispered something in her ear and she threw back her head and laughed raucously, drawing curious looks. The coloured lights from the DJ's desk threw her face into sharp relief, highlighting unusual planes and angles, making her look suddenly old. They touched her blonde hair with an unexpected red.

The song swirled to a close and the couple slipped away into the darkness. Robert quietly padded after them. The DJ pumped up the volume of the theme tune for a beer commercial and the lights fell into sync, spattering the crowd with rainbow-coloured circles. For a brief, panicky moment, Robert lost sight of Karen and the rugby player. Then he glimpsed a flash of red hair moving into the night.

Robert desperately wanted to walk away, to forget what he was seeing, to forget Karen, to go home and go to bed, to wake up in the morning and discover that it had all been a dream. Nothing more than a dream. He had never wanted anything so much in his life. "This is madness," he said aloud, unaware that he had spoken.

But still he followed them.

Away from the lights of the disco the night had grown surprisingly dark. The pulse and throb of the music faded as Robert followed the couple. Squinting hard, he attempted to keep them in sight, but they were moving quickly and confidently down an almost pitch-dark path. He wondered how they could see so well. Faintly, the boy's voice drifted back to him, asking something. It sounded high-pitched and maybe just a little alarmed.

Abruptly Robert stumbled and fell on the lightless path, crashing to the ground and skinning the palms of both hands. As he lay on the earth, he bit down hard on the inside of his cheek so he wouldn't cry out. He heard the couple ahead of him stop, and again the young man's voice was raised in a question. Then they moved on.

As silently as possible Robert got to his feet, ignoring the pain in his hands, and followed them.

He found the couple in the shadow of the bathing shelter. Crouching down, he spotted them dimly outlined against the sea only a few yards away from him, standing so close together they looked almost like one person with two heads. Karen giggled . . . not the light, happy giggle she'd used with him, but a different sound, a knowing, smirking sort of laugh. Ugly. Not like the girl he loved at all.

Robert didn't realise that he was crying until he tasted the salt on his lips. Angrily, he brushed a sleeve across his eyes. In the same moment he heard a gasp . . . of shock . . . of pain. It was followed by a terrible rattling gurgle.

His rubber-soled sneakers made no sound on the grass. He was almost on top of the couple before they were aware of him. He caught a glimpse of Karen's face, bone white in the starlight – except that it wasn't Karen's face. It was as if something were wearing a tissue-thin mask of her face, with the original features still visible beneath.

Robert turned toward the rugby player only to find him lying slumped against the wall, eyes closed, mouth open, a dark scarf draped carelessly around his neck. But this was the middle of summer, nobody needed a . . .

He realised that he wasn't looking at a scarf in the same instant the girl lunged for him, a flash of white in her hands. He tumbled forward, slithering on seaweed, falling headfirst into the youth, the two of them sprawled together in a tangle of limbs.

Karen towered over them, then suddenly struck down with the semi-circular white object in her hand. The force of the blow was extraordinary. Robert felt the body atop him shudder. He rolled, trying to use the other boy as a shield, as she struck again. He felt something sharp sink deep into the crook of his arm. Like a bite. He wrenched his arm away and heard the object clatter to the ground.

The girl screamed.

The sound rose, soaring higher and higher, a terrible howl of rage that dripped hate and hunger. On and on it went, tearing the air in a steady ululation.

All across Skerries dogs began to howl, and cats to hiss and spit.

One by one the disco lights exploded, showering the dancers with white-hot shards of glass. Glass bottles of minerals and lemonade started trembling, then shattered.

Cans burst, spewing liquid high into the air. All across the town, car and house alarms came to shrieking life.

The creature who had been Karen O'Sullivan ceased her own howling and stooped and grabbed for Robert, who was desperately trying to scramble out from under the body of her first victim. Robert's nose and ears were bleeding. He had actually heard his ears pop when Karen started screaming.

But this wasn't Karen. He knew that now. He knew what she had become.

When she reached for him, instinct made him strike upwards with the object he had snatched off the ground. He felt it thud against something solid.

Karen hissed with pain . . . and some other, less identifiable emotion, then turned and vanished into the night.

Trembling and nauseated, Robert sat up and looked at the object in his hand.

He was holding the bone comb he had discovered in the churchyard. The comb he had given to Karen.

The puzzle almost made sense now. And one final truth emerged: if it started with the comb he had given the girl . . . then he was to blame.

CHAPTER
THIRTY-ONE

Frustration lent her strength. She clawed her way through the last few handfuls of stone and earth in a frenzy. A straight-fingered punch into the darkness drove her arm deep into the soil, crumbling rocks and earth . . . and then her fingers wriggled free.

She had been close, so close!

She had almost complete control of the girl now. It had been a simple matter for her to select one of the human kind – she had deliberately chosen someone who looked strong and healthy – and then even easier to draw him away into the shadows.

Strega hadn't had this much control when she first sent her creature, the girl known as Ka-rin, out to hunt for her. Strega had plucked the image of the youth called Pa-trix El-es from Ka-rin's mind and guided her to him. But the girl's will had been strong, and she had struggled against Strega's command, forcing her to lose control at the crucial moment. The boy had overbalanced and toppled into the sea before she had a chance to feed. What a waste.

The next night when Strega had sent her out, her

control was already much more complete. That tiny portion of Ka-rin's mind which remained human had been horrified and revolted as Strega made her plunge the comb into the unsuspecting dogs, but she'd been unable to do anything about it. The comb had drunk deeply through its nine teeth, briefly turning a deep, almost mahogany-coloured brown before Strega had absorbed the accumulated essence in the Dreamscape.

But this night she had meant to feast on human blood.

Digging her way, wormlike, out of the coffin was exhausting, even for someone with her extraordinary strength. An infusion of human blood would give her the strength to continue. She had actually taken the boy, had already driven the comb into his throat when the boy Roburt had appeared and ruined everything.

Pulling herself free of the hole, Strega dropped down into a damp, foul-smelling room. She landed easily on her hands and knees and crouched there, nostrils flaring, eyes narrowing to tiny slits as she surveyed the shadows, taking in the shape of the room.

She was in a crypt, a burial chamber. This must lie below the chapel, and had obviously been built long after she was buried. The place was bitterly cold, and stank of mould and ancient decay. Generations of brittle rat bones crackled beneath her bare feet with every step, and she could hear the red-eyed creatures chittering in the darkness.

Strega smiled. This was good . . . very good. In fact this was perfect. The perfect end to an imperfect night.

Her smile broadened. She had meant to drink human

blood tonight. She had meant to do it through the comb which had been shaped from her father's thigh bones. But why indulge in a feast second-hand . . . when she could do it properly?

Closing her eyes, she called the creature she now controlled to her.

And licked her lips in anticipation.

CHAPTER THIRTY-TWO

One shouldn't feel actual pain in a dream. Even in the worst of nightmares, it shouldn't hurt. But why then did she have this terrible pain in her chest? The long muscles in her thighs were on fire and her feet pounding the pavement felt like she was running on broken glass.

Karen wanted this dream to end. She wanted to wake up. She desperately wanted to wake up. Unconsciously, the girl running down the middle of the road started to cry: solemn, blood-red tears.

Robert had "borrowed" a bike to try and keep up with Karen, a mountain bike, eighteen speeds, with fat, wide-bodied tyres. By experiment, he had worked out the proper combination of gears and was already travelling far too fast to be comfortable. There was no light on the bike and the front brake pads were missing. But even pedalling furiously in top gear, he was unable to catch up with her. He could just about make her out in the distance. She was running with a long, loping stride . . . and as she ran beneath the street lights, they exploded into dust above her head.

But he knew he didn't have to catch up with her . . . he had a very good idea where she was going. Back to where it started. Back to Baldungan Castle.

If Karen followed the usual route to the castle she would simply go through the town, then down the long, almost straight road until she came to the cross-roads in Loughshinny, then turn right up Featherbed Lane.

He knew he was not going to be able to catch up with her – even with the bike. They hadn't even left the town and already he was breathing hard. There was another route to the castle up along the Golf-Links Road, a dangerously narrow, twisting country road, with no street lights. But it was shorter.

Her entire body was on fire.

It began in her lungs, a searing white heat that scorched her throat with every breath. The same fire burned her feet, seared her calves and thighs, making every step an agony. Her head was pounding, every step making it worse.

She wanted to stop, to lie down and sleep.

Could she sleep in a dream?

Was this a dream?

Lights appeared before her, blinding and terrifying. The monster roared, the sounds spiralling down through her consciousness until she recognised it as a car horn beeping furiously at her. She kept running, moving straight into the light, inexorably pulled in that direction. She was hardly even aware of the shattering of glass and metal as the car swerved and smashed into a lamppost.

She was coming.

Strega moved around the crypt, calloused, black-nailed feet slithering across the floor.

Waiting.

She could feel her creature coming, drawing slowly, steadily nearer. If the vampyre closed her eyes she could almost see the bright thread of blood approaching, could almost taste the meaty warmth on her lips.

She drove a fist through the stout wooden door, the only entrance into the crypt. Dry wood exploded into sawdust, the door swayed on leather hinges and then tore free to crash into the room. In the confines of the small chamber the noise was deafening.

Trembling with excitement, the vampyre crawled up the narrow stone steps.

Robert was beginning to think that taking this route was a mistake. It might have been shorter, but riding a bike on a twisting country road was a deadly undertaking. He'd already fallen twice. Once when something – it might have been a cat or a large rat – had run right under his tyres and squealed terribly, and then again, a few moments later, when he'd misjudged a corner and cycled straight into a ditch.

But he knew he simply had to get to the castle because he was beginning to suspect that someone – or something – would be waiting for Karen there.

He kept seeing the image of a girl with red hair.

She'd lost her shoes and was now running in her bare feet, leaving perfect impressions of the soles of her feet in blood on the road behind her. She was aware that there was blood on her face, trickling from her nose; she could taste it on her upper lip. She had fallen more than once. For the few moments she had been lying on the ground she had found herself crawling, pulling her body along with her ragged, bloody fingernails, using raw elbows and skinned knees to propel herself forward.

She wanted to stop.

But she couldn't stop.

She was going to run until her heart burst.

A clenched fist burst through the floor, shattering stone, sending pebbles scattering everywhere. Strega enlarged the opening with her head and shoulders, prying away more chunks of stone as she opened the long forgotten entrance to the crypt. Crawling out, she found she was under the tower, the last remnant of the original chapel. The vampyre smiled, long teeth glinting; she remembered this tower being built more than six hundred years ago.

Striding across to the modern metal gate that prevented unauthorised access to the tower, she wrapped her hands around the thick padlock, and twisted. The padlock shattered in her hands. Pulling open the gate with enough force to wrench it from the walls, Strega retreated to the crypt, the remnants of her white gown dragging behind her.

Soon.

Soon she would feast.

CHAPTER
THIRTY-THREE

He was too late.

He could see Karen ahead of him. She was crossing the field, heading towards the ruined chapel. She was moving slowly, jerkily, like a puppet with broken strings. With the last of his energy Robert stood on the pedals and sent the bike surging forwards.

But by the time he reached the entrance to the field, Karen had disappeared.

He was climbing over the metal gate when his hand came away sticky. He held it up; his fingers appeared black in the faint light. Red appears black at night, he knew. He was looking at Karen's blood.

Bent double with a stitch in his side and stomach cramps, Robert staggered across the field, wishing he had enough breath left to call out.

The pain, the terrible pain in her bloody feet, torn hands and knees and elbows, finally drove the last of the dream away. This was no dream, this was a terrible, terrifying reality.

Karen knew where she was, know how she had got

here, knew also what she had done over the past few days. It was as if a veil had been lifted off her eyes, allowing her to see clearly.

And now she was standing here, in an ancient crypt.

Waiting.

Waiting while something moved in the darkness, watching with a gaze so intense she could actually feel it. Karen knew what waited in the darkness; it had inhabited her thoughts and dreams over the past few days. She felt she knew the creature as it must know her.

"I am Strega," said the voice, echoing in the chamber. "I am the last of the Sith."

Thick candles hissed into life. They exuded a bitter odour that send Karen stumbling back, and when she looked at them more closely she realised they were not candles at all. They were human thigh bones.

The red-haired woman was standing in the centre of a circle formed by the bizarre candles. Her eyes shifted, pupils narrowing to slits then flaring as they fixed on the girl's terrified face, like a serpent mesmerising a bird. The Sith's red hair began to shift, first individual strands moving, then whole tresses rising to flow out in an unfelt breeze.

Karen's lips moved. "You . . . you made me do all those things."

"I dreamed them. *You* did them." She held out her hands commandingly. "Come to me."

Karen shook her head violently, but her torn feet stepped forward.

"Why me?" She was too tired even to cry, too sick to care.

The vampyre raised her fingers to her red hair. "Because we are linked, you and I." She lifted a comb, a twin of the one Robert had given Karen four days ago. Was it only four days? It seemed like a lifetime.

"Once the comb had tasted your blood . . . you were mine," the creature said.

Unconsciously Karen touched her neck where she'd scratched it with the comb. She remembered being surprised that there had been so little blood.

"I had intended to feed through you," the vampyre went on, "until I had regained my full strength, but now those plans have changed. I have decided to feed *off* you instead."

With violently trembling hands, Karen made the sign of the Cross.

The vampyre merely laughed. "Your magical signs have no power over me. I was in Jerusalem when they hung him on a cross between a pair of thieves. I saw no miracles." Crossing her fingers, she called Karen forward another step. "You will be the first human blood I have tasted in more than half a century. Oh, I enjoyed the dogs' blood, but it is like thin and bitter vinegar compared to the nectar of human blood."

"And then what?" Karen asked desperately, determined to keep the conversation going as long as possible. While they spoke, at least she was still alive.

Strega's smile was savage. "Your blood will give me enough strength to hunt for a little more. Once I have drunk of the blood of three adult humans, I will have regained the peak of my powers."

Karen was unwillingly dragged another step closer,

almost to the edge of the blazing bones. "Once my people ruled the world, but then fear and superstition drove us underground. Now I am about to establish a new reign of the Sith in this world. You should be honoured that you have been chosen. When the future history of the world comes to be written, your name will go down alongside mine." Strega smiled. "Fame . . . of a sort. A pity you will not be able to enjoy it."

Reaching out, she grabbed Karen by the shoulders, pulling her forward. The girl screamed and struggled, but the vampyre's grip was like iron. Karen looked up into a mouthful of ragged teeth, watched as the incisors grew, lengthening into fangs. A forked tongue flickered out, licking at the flesh of Karen's neck, tasting the salt sweat.

And Robert plunged the comb into the vampyre's throat.

The creature lunged away from Karen with a hideous scream, flailing out, sending the boy flying into one of the burning bones. Hungry flames caught at the edge of his coat and began to smoulder.

On hands and knees, face covered by the mass of red hair, still screaming, the vampyre crawled towards him. The bone comb was still stuck in her back. He could see the comb visibly pulsing, throbbing, changing colour, swelling as it sucked her blood.

The raging vampyre slashed furiously at him, ragged nails tearing strips from his jeans but not touching his flesh.

Strega reared over him, suddenly howling afresh, and half turned . . . Robert saw that Karen had plunged one of the burning bones into the creature's leg. The vampyre turned on her, claws extended into daggers.

Without thinking, Robert launched himself at the creature. He landed on her back, the force of his weight driving the bone comb deeper into the creature's spine. Then suddenly the comb shattered, spraying him with a fine, gritty red powder.

Strega howled, desperately trying to reach around to the back of her neck. When she opened her mouth, the sound that emerged was like nothing that had ever issued from a human throat. It was the sound of primal evil.

With the last of his strength, Robert stepped past the flailing vampyre. He looked into Karen's face, saw his own terror mirrored there, and knew then that she had come back to him. Grabbing her by the arm, he pulled her away . . .

. . . as Strega wrapped her fist in Karen's hair.

Robert snatched one of the bone candles and used its dancing flame to sear and crisp the blond hair held in the vampyre's clutch. The burning strands parted, setting Karen free.

The hair remaining in the vampyre's hands was blazing as she slumped among the rat bones in the crypt, but she seemed unaware of it. Lines and traceries of colour appeared on her skin, swirling patterns, intricate curls, ornate designs etched in blue.

Both Karen and Robert recognised the patterns from the comb.

The fire that burned in the vampyre's hands now crept up the sleeve of her gown, but she ignored it. She was clawing at her face, at the patterns that were now spreading, turning her pale flesh blue.

With a tremendous effort Strega came to her feet and

lunged for Karen and Robert. If she could just taste blood – just a single drop! – it would reverse the process.

She knew what was happening. The comb, the drinking comb, shaped from her father's bones; the comb that had drunk the blood of countless thousands down through the ages, sucking the living essence of the human kind, was now drinking her essence, sucking the life from her.

Each line on the comb, every line now appearing etched in the pattern on her face, spoke of a human life taken.

All she needed was a single drop of blood.

She lurched towards the couple.

The girl screamed and the boy pushed her away into the shadows. Strega lunged for him. Rat bones crumbled beneath her feet, throwing her off balance. She fell against a pillar, wrapping her arms around it. Old stone cracked and shuddered . . . and gave.

And the room caved in with a tremendous roar.

E P I L O G U E

In the ruins of Baldungan Castle, something stirred. Rocks shifted, clattered, pebbles rattled. A single white arm appeared, fingers moving slowly towards the light. A second arm appeared, and then a head, white with dust and grit.

A girl crawled out of the wreckage, stood and shook the dust from her hair. In the pre-dawn light, the hair gleamed blond.

Reaching into the hole in the ground, she dragged the boy out, then knelt to cradle his head in her lap. He groaned and attempted to open his eyes.

"Is it over?" Robert whispered, voice raw with dust and terror.

"It's over," Karen said simply.

"Are you sure? How can you tell?"

She smiled down at him. "I can tell."

"No more dreams?"

"They've gone," she lied.